I want to thank everyone
I love everybody who hates me
and I love everyone who loves me

!!!!!!!!!!!!!!!!

© ordineri

Cover Art in cooperation with Darius Harder and Jessica Kraft
Special Thanks to Lennard „Lenny" Matthias Szpunar

ordineri on ordineri 7
early stage 10
    pleasure 11
    table dance 12
      running circles 13
    Fall 14
    Messages 15
    Games 16
    Floor (light acid episode) 17
    why did you forget trash bag? 18
    <3 <3 <3 19
    Mamma Mia 22
    chained up 23
    Fuck freedom 24
    r.i.p sigmund freud 25
    long way 26
    remeniscing 27
    Observation Pt. II. 29
    Last halloween 30
    lost 31
    work 32
    the trouble with being born 33
    present tense 34
    short night tweaking on 2cb (kanye west tribute) 35
    nuances of sex 36
    I fried my brain in berlin 37
    Observation (speed dating in berlin) 38
    a questionaire (???) 39
    sinning PRO edition 40
    work at work 41
    first snow 44
    what I'm missing 45
    easy door metaphor 47
    result of my field studies 48
    cute date idea 49
    a short love story 50
    light digestable philosophy 51
    peach 53
    always be open to new experiences 54
    Tuesday night's 55
    restart 56
    jesus christ 57
    same old shit 58
failed visa experience 60
    Destiny 61
    mosquito repellant 62

Hello	63
island shopping	64
the scooter and the gods	65
the guru's birthday	66
the balls (if you don't read till end you'll think I'm an asshole but I'm actually a very sensitive poet)	67
Emergency	69
a real poem	70
the young germans	71
back home	73
lone ranger in pseudo isolation	74
sex next to the kitchen	75
my wishlist for christmas	76
basic bitch motivational quote/ig caption	77
when I'm at home	78
Damage limitation	79
When done	81
days and days	82
Faking it	83
Edgy love poem	85
silence	86
simple dog doing tricks	87
edible	88
tinder covid simulation/roulette	89
Aliens	91
all we do is get fucked	93
Evolution	94
Revolution	95
A lost day	96
good kids bad kids	97
hotbox in a forest	98
Waiting for the train	99
craving	100
it's time	101
the waitress	102
riding bikes all day	103
Letter_for_a_girl.mp3	104
Fair play	105
I was done and took a last puff	106
human interaction	107
beauty and perfection	109
A vague love poem	110
Sometimes hate	111
Tomato titty	113
Two ways to win an argument	114
fomo	115

- chaotic arrangement of words ... 116
- Whatsapp poem ... 117
- summer sweat ... 118
- Dirty dancing ... 119
- Toxic masculinity ... 120
- inside ... 121
- too dumb to suffer ... 122
- blue hair pink pill ... 123
- Nervous ... 124
- Sunday ... 125
- roundabout ... 126
- Life hack 1 ... 129
- Low end real as fuck shit ... 130
- the sun made me soft ... 131
- foreplay ... 133
- Salty but sweet liquid ... 134
- silver fish metaphor ... 135
- extra soberness ... 136
- A picture ... 137
- A starry night ... 138
- A day ... 139
- Highest highs Lowest lows ... 140
- Life hack 2 ... 141
- the belly button ... 142
- disinfection ... 143
- Last time i painted ... 144
- The legends ... 145
- fear of commitment ... 146
- Why I love whores ... 147
- peaking ... 148
- Identity ... 149
- Preach ... 150
- dignity ... 151
- BLIND!!!!!!!!! ... 152
- Smalltalk ... 153
- Pesto-Pasta ... 154
- Playing scrabble in the garden and drinking liquor ... 155
- schönheit ... 156
- When talking becomes redundant ... 157
- Steady simpin' ... 158
- Friction ... 159
- The mirror ... 160
- Frog shit ... 161
- internalization ... 162
- working long happy hours ... 163
- Conversation with god ... 164

- Love <3 165
- Party Paradox 166
- uncanny observations 167
- realization of my last acid trip 168
- irresponsibility and heartbreak 169
- Waves of sobering intoxication 170
- painting date 171
- Why you should pee with an open door 172
- the fall 174
  - nipple fever 175
  - omw to the metro 177
  - philosophy of quality 178
  - Thanks mother nature 179
  - perspective 180
  - Modern romance 181
  - short precarious glance 182
  - dans la provence 183
  - when the dog chased its tail 185
  - the color 186
  - Degeneration 187
  - decent humans 190
  - The contrary of foreplay 191
  - giving love/preserving love 192
  - Fingering with tobacco fingers 193
  - brahman way of creating 194
  - Practise 195
  - Unprecedented sympathy and remorse 196
  - In summer 197
  - window 199
  - the rose & the virgin 200
  - in the bus on the way to get my charger 204
  - Kawasaki sperm 205
  - speaking with my father 207
  - cemetery 208
  - studying 209
  - random impact 211
  - contradiction 212
  - the longest night of the year 213
  - tic tac toe 215
  - colours 216
  - highway romance 217
  - the fauteuil 218
  - silence with each other 219
  - extra 219
  - Money 220
- New year New me 222

high in school	223
silence ended in reciprocal agreement	225
without being stated as something	225
wordly things should describe	225
Cash Money Poem	227
baby producing process simulation accident	228
The holistic approach	229
Sunscreen*	231
at the metro	233
experiences shape the mind	234
animals and humans in comparison	235
superstition	236
a political dream (utopy)	237
religion	239
When I was 14 I had to shoot a dog	240
Imaginary conversation with butter	241
some words to my dad in english that he will never read but i make him feel with my actions in his presence	243
Peer pressure and standardization	244
dancing in the moon light	245
In a room	246
Love	247
Hate (projected from the inside outside)	248
The crying episode	249
the worst thing	250
Don't throw this away!	251
How beautiful	252

ARE YOU THE PROTAGONIST OF YOUR OWN LIFE?

Introduction
ordineri on ordineri

This volume of poems deals with experiences, perceptions, and arousals that happened to me over the course of the last one and a half years.

It is a small gift, a gift that must be gifted because oneself has been gifted a gift as well.
It is a balancing act between the compulsive attempt at capturing the essence of life again and again, and encapsulating the consciousness that I witnessed, for the world that is to come.

A gift that one has often been gifted, just as I have found tempestuous consolation within great works, on leaden nights.

It's time to give something back.
I am a child of my time, and all carnal ideals derive from the process of all preceding eras in history.

It would be a lie to state that our ideas are more modern, more noble, more important, more holistic, since the human is not more than a simple animal, predictable since Shakespeare and Moliere; dissected and preserved within their own great works.

And yet it's important to recognize the contemporary moral, to incorporate one's own impulses and demands into the inexhaustible path of time, for the sake of walking, to extend the travel, to enrich the traveller.

It's a big task and you have to feel worthy.
The title in itself is a metaphor.
Two words that have only been given a shape in recent internet history are the basic polarizing/bipolar feelings in the modern human, the consequences they experience in the course of the masked game as a part of society.

The music alternates between cheerful and gloomy, although we more often find ourselves singing about the blueness of the sky rather than weeping over the greyness of the storm.

Even the valley of despair sees itself as salvation, as a glimpse that one catches on the other side, as the salvation of being allowed to feel the shadows rather than having to fear them, for a three dimensional experience of our time.

original essay translated by cameron lee f. (@yakkainacam)

early stage

CERTAINTY

I KNOW I'LL DIE
I KNOW IT WONT BE
TOMORROW

PLEASURE

I SMOKED A CIGARETTE
ON MOMA
THAT WAS THE BEST THING
I EVER DID IN MY LIFE

I SMOKED A JOINT
WHILE SHITTING
THAT WAS THE BEST THING
I EVER DID IN MY LIFE

I FUCKED MY FIRST LOVE
ON ACID
THAT WAS THE BEST THING
I EVER DID IN MY LIFE

table dance

somebody broke the table
it was made of glass
and put mushrooms
in my soup

the waitress serves beer
they smoke inside
I want to be like them
so I drink up

they long for death
await the life
it makes no sense
I grab her by the ass
and laugh
nobody made a joke

running circles

IT ALL MAKES SENSE
LOVE AND HATE ARE ONLY
SEPERATED BY A THIN LINE

HURTING A LOVED ONE
IS HURTING YOURSELF

WE ARE SEPERATED
BY OUR BODIES
BUT BREATH
THE SAME AIR

SLEEPING NAKED
PLAYING CHESS
RUNNING CIRCLES
THE GAME IS SO HARD
TO PLAY

Fall

A sweet little face
A sweet round butt
It's getting cold
But lips and pussy
Keep me comfy

Again and again
it doesn't matter
who the fish is
or the fisherman

I sit on the grass
as long as I can
and smoke my cigarette
in the sun light

Messages

She wants me to suffer
She wants to sit on my
face
She wants me to wait
to really ride it
all out

I don't know how serious
She is about it
But I guess I'll find out
I really need to get
in there again
to get home

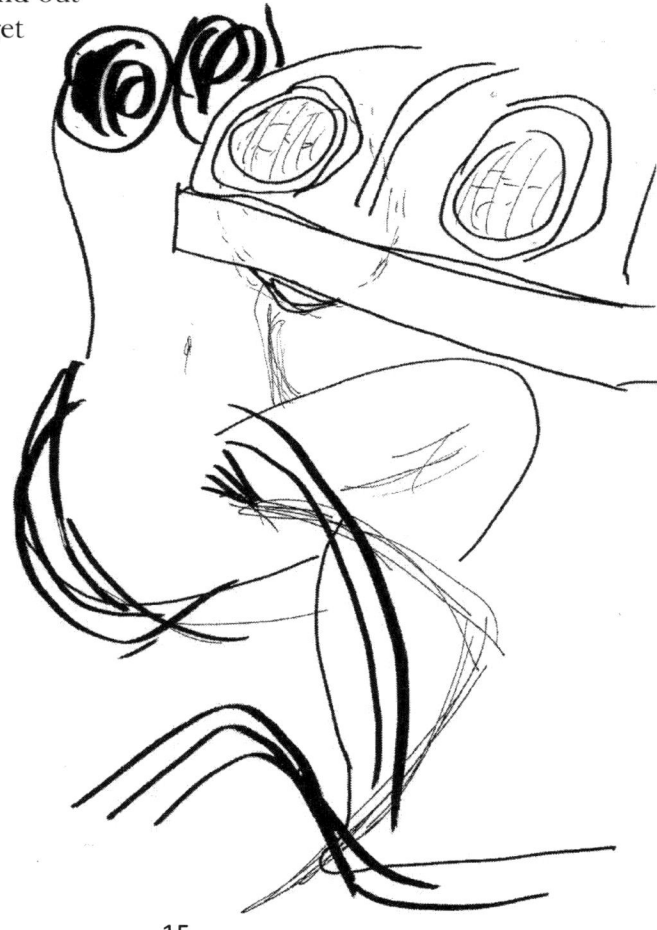

Games

Life gets difficult
when you have options
and even then
play it cool
let it go
but again
what do you want?

Not seeing the step
breaking my toe
it was worth it
it always is

Making each other
jealous
to prove something
when there is just us
everybody goes home
as a loser

Floor (light acid episode)

You know that I like
this kind of surprise
you motherfucker
knew all the way

Ash on the floor
just don't let it ....
but it felt so good ....
Sometimes you speak
about topics
which are silent

Asking questions
for the question
not for the answer

why did you forget trash bag?

> WHY DID YOU FORGET TRASH BAG
>
> WHY DID YOU FORGET THE FIRST TIME YOU OPENED A ~~BOOK~~ BOTTLE
>
> WHEN WAS THE LAST
>
> YOU STARTED GOING TO THE TOILET ALONE YOU EARNED IT
>
> BUT VHY DID FORGET THE TRASHBAG

its's super cold, I'm freezing

Oh baby

Didn't you get the memo?
it's cuffing season
all singles are miserable
and everybody who found somebody
is happy
as long as they don't have to
                          sleep alone

Oh honey
Didn't you watch the news?
People who have "ACAB" tattooed
                        on their bodies
call the police
when they are threatened

cold shower thoughts

if you don't
    believe in anything
   you have freedom

but if you don't
    believe in anything

   you have no reason

<3 <3 <3

WHEN YOU SLIDE
YOUR MIDDLEFINGER IN

LOOK EACH OTHER
IN THE EYE
AND IT GETS SO TIGHT
IT FEELS LIKE
YOUR FINGER IS STUCK

THAT'S LOVE

Mamma Mia

She gives me a
„ciao bello"
I am just happy
What a beautiful
day
to die

But not yet
I have to find out
what is
on the other side

chained up

They hold each others hand
but they sit on the man's lap
both look out of the window
in opposite directions

Happy faces, I see none
just unquestioned ideas
that take roots in bitter lips
and shallow eyes

Arriving at the destination
anxiously leaving the seats
they warmed up
looking back
but they are not theirs anymore

Fuck freedom

FUCK FREEDOM
YOUR SWEET WORDS
YOUR SWEET FACE
MAKE ME A
FUCKING SLAVE

I FEEL BAD
AND I LOVE IT

r.i.p sigmund freud

Let love be love

Let's not fuck each other over
Because suffering is suffering
And loving is loving
Suffering for love
No, it's sufferung for a
weird idea you try to project
in a human

Don't bring presents
If you want something in return

long way

we went from fucking as friends
to fucking as lovers
from fucking in the forest
to fucking on acid

we went from fucking
on the toilet in a filthy club
to fucking as emotionally
fully developed adults

we went from fucking as strangers
to not fucking at all

Now I beg the beggar
to take my money
But he refuses
„it is too late" (he laughs)

But you know,
I'll always love you, bitch

remeniscing

I remember having fistfights
over words, over insults
over pride and nationality.

I remember being angry
and punching the soft kids
at school.

I remember stealing
sweets and shoes.
First because we were poor
but then for the rush

I remember sleeping bad
lying awake over a
mistake, being devoured
by the consequences that'll
face me tomorrow

I remember fucking friends
over for a gram

I remember laughin at
people when they cried

I remember being a little
dumbfuck who wouldn't
understand why people act
in certain ways, only
relying on the things they
say

I remember being shitless
scared when these 4
golems were waiting for
me outisde. And I remember
getting jumped by them later

All this while I sit next to
this beautiful confusion
All this while I grip
her thigh and smell
her hair

Observation Pt. II

A man walks to a woman
it is loud, but they still
manage to talk

He goes to the bar, confident
and is followed by her
the conversation
is followed by a cheeky
little smile
and a subtle, gentle touch

The fella is going for it
the drinks are coming
she takes hers, turns away
and hints at a sudden
escape
He leans forward, angrily
his friends hold him back

......and she is gone
disappeared on the dance floor........

Last halloween

I wasn't really drunk
I wasn't really dressed
I was out there, alone
and saw this girl
with big tiddies
who I knew

We walked and drank
I invited her back to my place
She has her period
She said
Ok, said I
We won't fuck, she said
Ok said I

From festivity to bedroom
From kissing to eating pussy
From clean to dirty
I don't like the idea
of taboo
Neither am I scared of
                blood
But she left her tampon
right beside the pillow

lost

lost
lost
lost
when you're lost
you sense
that everybody
is lost

You see it
in every glance
and hear it
in every word

Let's close the distance
and get lost together
beautiful
meaningless
freedom

work

I got no money on my mind
but I got money in my pocket
I sacrifice my time
for security
and independence

PARADOX

Independent of my family
Dependent of my job
Safeplace security
is just another word for fear
Fear of the unknown outisde world

Yeah
But I jack off at work
and still get paid
Fuck capitalism right?

the trouble with being born

THE WORST PART
ABOUT BEING A HUMAN
IN MODERN SOCIETY
IS

NOT BEING ABLE
TO TAKE A SHIT
WHEN YOU FEEL
THE URGE
BUT HAVING TO
FIND A TOILET FIRST

present tense

HARD TO COMPREHEND
THAT WE ARE A PART OF THE
LIFE OF EVERY PERSON WE
SHARE THE PRESENT WITH

(THAT EVERYBODY HAS IT'S
OWN THOUGHTS)

AND WE DON'T TRY TO MAKE
THE BEST OUT OF IT

short night tweaking on 2cb (kanye west tribute)

That feeling
When nobody can give you what you want
Except you
Yourself through somebody
Or something????

nuances of sex

SEX IS COOL
BUT SLOWLY
RUNNING YOUR FINGER
UP HER THIGH
BARELY
TOUCHING IT
FEELING IT
TWITCH
IN SUPPRESSED EXCITEMENT
IS ALSO NICE :)

I fried my brain in berlin

SOFT LIPS
SOFT CHEEKS
SOFT BUTTOCKS
SOFT TOUCHES
HARD DRUGS
HARD TOUCHES
HARD HARD-ON

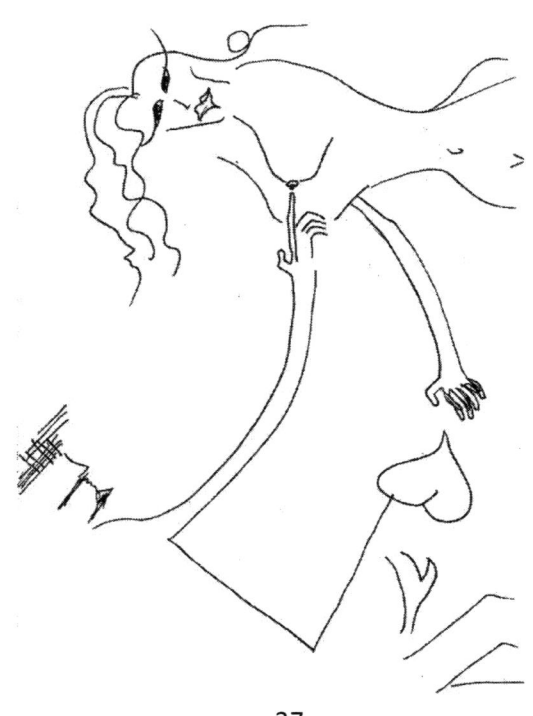

Observation (speed dating in berlin)

7am, blasting music
let's the clothes
on your skin (((tremble)))

A guy, with a sharp face
shows his notebook
to a girl

Everything was drawn
with a thick marker
It had heart
but seemed clumsy

The girl turnes some pages
then shakes her head
in a superior manner

She pulls out her phone
and displays her pieces
on instagram

„I drew that" her lips moved
silently
HYPERREALISTIC PENCIL DRAWINGS OF
FACES AND FLOWER

a questionaire (???)

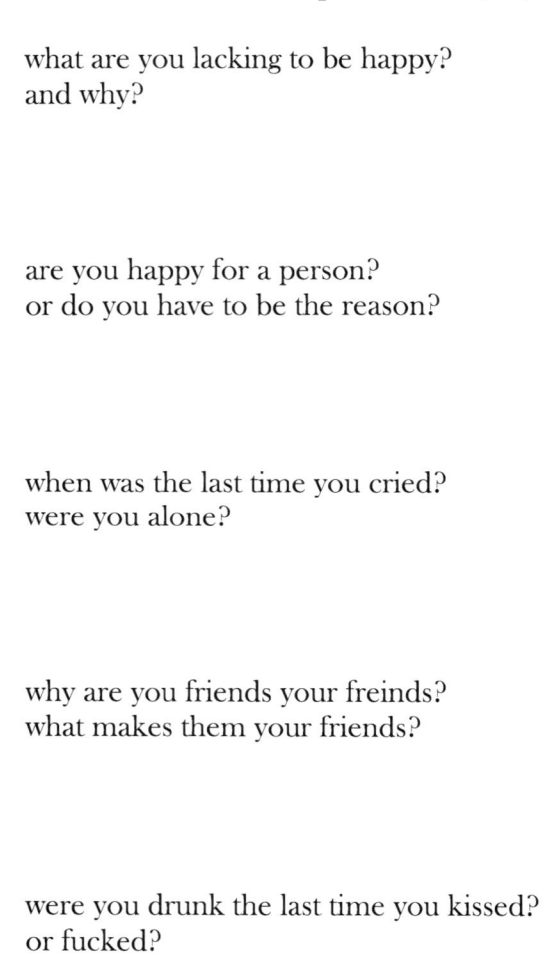

what are you lacking to be happy?
and why?

are you happy for a person?
or do you have to be the reason?

when was the last time you cried?
were you alone?

why are you friends your freinds?
what makes them your friends?

were you drunk the last time you kissed?
or fucked?

sinning PRO edition

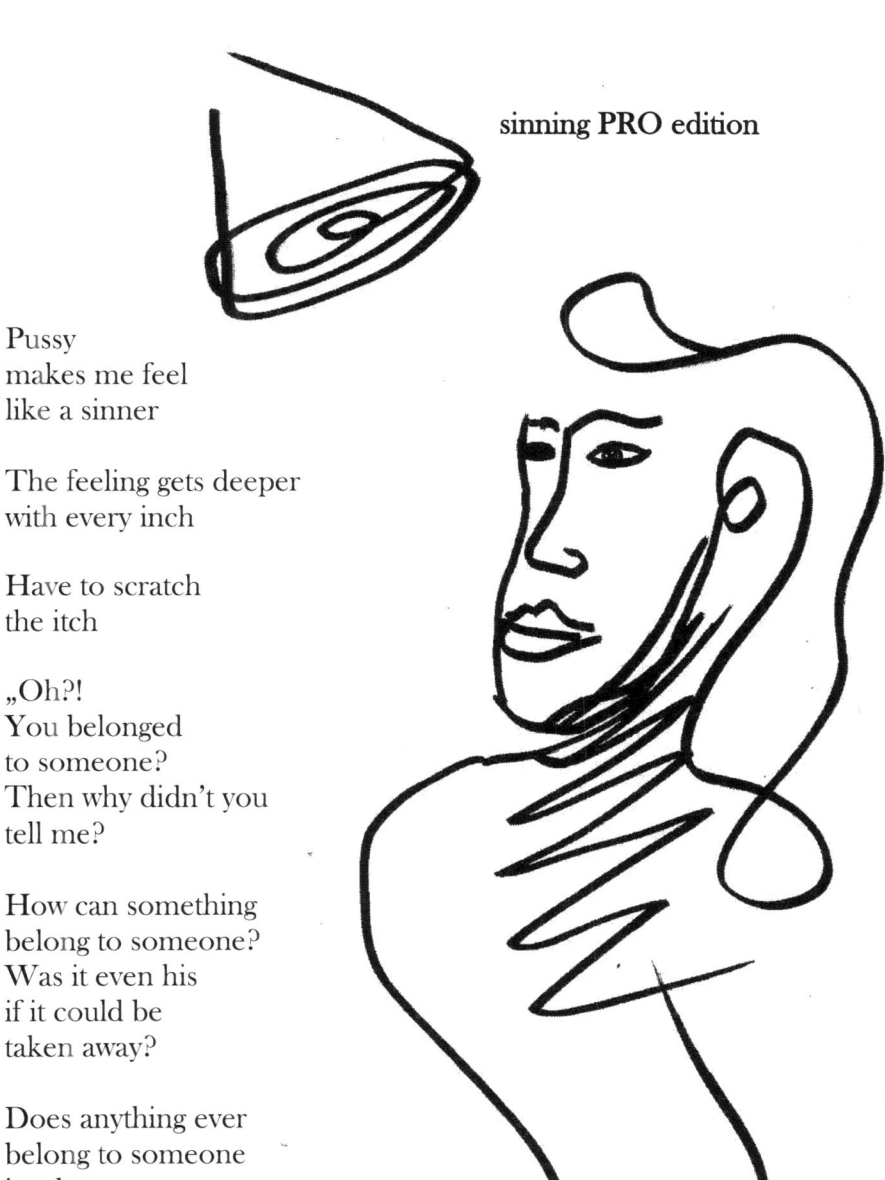

Pussy
makes me feel
like a sinner

The feeling gets deeper
with every inch

Have to scratch
the itch

„Oh?!
You belonged
to someone?
Then why didn't you
tell me?

How can something
belong to someone?
Was it even his
if it could be
taken away?

Does anything ever
belong to someone
just because
you paid a price
for it?"

work at work

„Please don't forget it"
(it seems to be important)
OK
take all
the needed precautions
focus
focus
feetus, fetus
fuck
I lost control
and can't stop
but the doctor
said it's fine
it's very normal
and the
    most
    important
it is organic
So don't you worry

Look how I'm
surfing on
my keyboard

It looks like fun
because it is
soaking wet
fun
but also
hard

CONCENTRATION

Don't think
anything
just stay still
still, still
still
calm

eat, fuck
sleep, dream
fuck, fuck, fuck
die, dead

2pm
the walls are
drenched
in moonlight
quiet
buzzing
steps
keys rattle
breathing
sitting
breathing seriously
rolling
scrolling

Look mom
I made it
the boss said
I'm a good
boy
    and
          gave
   me
      a treat

I am so content

first snow

Yesterday
I saw a woman
crying
the first snow
       was falling
But she didn't see it
as she stooped
       past me
inadvertently
       staring at her feet

At the metro
the snow was still falling
and as I minded
       my own business
A woman tackled me
trying to catch
snowflakes with her tongue

what I'm missing

I miss your sweet
       little face
and your lean body
your small tits
and your awkward smile
       (with the double chin)
your eyes that
       resembled
every cute animal
and your tight pussy

I miss getting high all day
       and fucking
             and sweating
and being the little
       spoon (sometimes)

I miss ignoring your texts
and randomly
       confessing my love
and telling you
       how beautiful
             you are

I miss your
        firm, round butt
and touching you
                in public

I miss you making
        me tea when
                I was
                      sick
        and calling
                me baby

I miss hearing about your day
while you undress
        and lay next to me
and sniffing your
                skin
like a fucking dog

easy door metaphor

opening doors
standing
      in the doorway
looking around
not being sure
wether you like it

opening the next
door
liking the last
      one better
checking it again
      it's closed

opening another
          door
going in
going out
closing doors

result of my field studies

People mostly talk about themselves and it reveals who they are

People don't like it when you interrupt and ask them something about themselves

cute date idea

Let's sit on the couch
while bossa nova jazz
is flooding the room
with only a dim light
in the corner

tell me about your passion
while you subtly touch
      my dick
but we both decide
      to ignore it
and play it cool
like grown-ups

a short love story

Our faces were separated
only by a thin wall
of air
It was either kissing her
or losing my mind
which is the same thing
eventually

„Do you wanna go to my place?"
„No, you can come to mine
but there won't be any
fucking going on tonight."

That was OK with me
it was chill
we finished the beers
and took the metro

„Don't be deceived by my
hard on. I really just
wanna kiss and cuddle."

She kept her word
and we made love
in the morning.

light digestable philosophy

it's obvious
do what you love
say what you think
take a little risk
let your true self
repel the phonies

try something new
make sacrifices
to know
if it is worth it

don't live as if you're going to
be reincarnated

don't search for
the meaning of life
outside of life

the worst thing I can imagine
is being 60
looking back at your life
and thinking
you could have done „it"
but you thought about
what other people might think
and have you ordinary life

don't let your yesterday
define your tomorrow
have a little freedom
be loyal to yourself
because the idea of life
will restrain you often enough

we're all humans for
the first time
nobody figured out
what it means to be
they only have
their limited beliefs
and habits

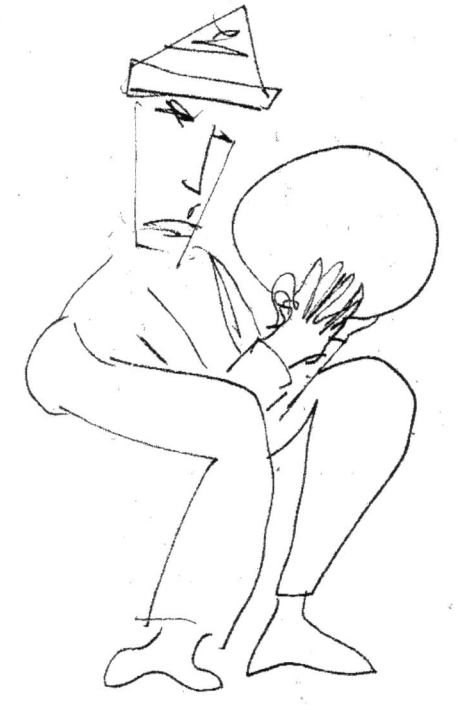

peach

FALLING IN
AND OUTTA LOVE
TWICE
A DAY

YOU TASTED
LIKE A SWEET PEACH
DIPPED IN COLD SALTY
SEA WATER
ON A ~~HOT~~ DAY
SUNNY

always be open to new experiences

you are the weird rich girl
the one who was obsessed
        with horses

The funny submissive girl
who would order water
      with every beer

We were sitting in the bathtub
you were brushing your teeth
and spat the toothpastefoam
        in the water

I was high as shit
      (trppy high)
trying to get a grip

Tuesday night's

You don't wanna go home alone
I don't wanna go home alone
but it's time to go home

yea let's split the bill
        emancipation

We have a couple numbers
              in our phones
but they are not the same
don't feel the same
don't taste the same
and it feels like love
but I know it is not

tomorrow I won't love you
                anymore
but I'll still love the
        moment
but you don't mind
and I wouldn't mind neither
because we'll be somewhere else
and love the moment
            or the people

restart

She deleted my number
Now it's in there again
How many reincarnations
will we need?

She said
She hates my guts
Now I'm in there again
in her guts

She said
Her relationship
just ended
But he never
        made her cum

I don't judge
I understand
I appreciate
        the honesty

jesus christ

fucking
with the devil

losing my mind

it's all blood
       and flesh

feel the sin

all pleasures
       are short-lived

sweat from face to face

no need to get
sentimental

just enjoy the ride

same old shit

The same empty words
The same busy streets
The same beautiful buildings
The same red wine
      but more

The same tasty tabacco
The same petty lies
The same disillusionmnet
and I say to myself
      „That's the last time
      I'm done."
      indifferently smiling

Going home to a
different set of cheeks
to small caring hands
to a soft loving face
and stupid dance moves
I'm a fool

I am a fool for
wanting something
          else

For thinking
    I want
        something else

But when I wake up
in my bed
alone
and the fairy
who brought me peace
is gone
I'll need another lie

failed visa experience

Destiny

„If it's meant to be it'll happen."

No, yo fucking dumbass
You can decide every moment
how you act
So it is your fault
      if it doenst

„Yeah, but in the end it's either
      YES or NO"

Yeah, you fucking donkey
but there are a million
different YES'es and NO's
      NUANCES

So I will take that into account
and appreciate the adversity
of life, calmly :)

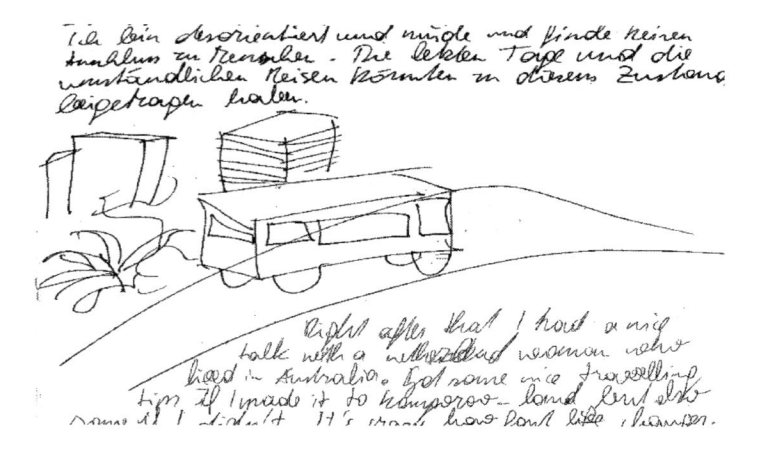

mosquito repellant

no mosquito repellant
everyone that travels
becomes a traveller
is no real person anymore

the two danish girls
travel with each other
because
one needs someone
       to go to the tourist attractions
the other one needs someone
       reliable
              for ig photos

I'm the edgy traveller
a different breed
I'm looking for [the story]

(not interested in superficial sex
or fucking temples)

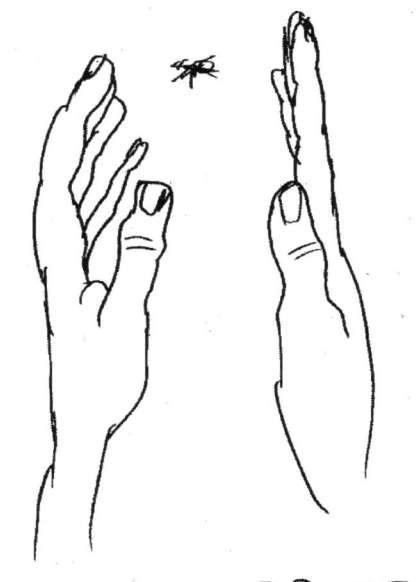

FUCKING MOZZIES

Hello

On the inside I'm clean
But on the outside I'm a dirty motherfucker
just filthy
My shirt reaks of sweat, saltwater
                               and 4 days
                                    4 days
                         2 humid days

The yoga teacher said alcohol and tabacco
                                     are poison
But that you can't get healthy
when you are sick in your head
She looked 4 years younger
                 than she was
You should've seen her ass

The old cross-eyes australian
told me of his luck
that he is not religous
but believes in jesus
something greater than himself

told me of his bad luck
breaking his neck twice
having H.I.V.

The gorgeous girl
tried to convince me
that she's not a basic bitch
after that remark slipped out of my mouth

But guess what ..... (she is)

island shopping

I bought a bird
On my way to the ATM
Out of the cage

The little bird
    was in my hands
I let it fly away

But I don't think it'll survive
I don't think it was meant
        to be free

the scooter and the gods

I love the idea of a god
even though if I can't sustain it

you're driving drunk
on your scooter
doing 70
and your helmet
saves your face
but the rest of the body
is just covered by clothing

you feel lightheaded
the wind in your face
you get excited
it's late
bumpy roads keep you alert

and you hope or might think
something's watching over you
maybe a god? maybe the universe?

Beer for Scooter
(LATE NIGHT EDITION)

the guru's birthday

It is the guru's birthday
over 100 people have gathered
I sit with the other 5 white people
and it is hard not to think
of it as a cult

To the left of me sits a big australian
probably 50 years old, maybe older
this guy punched people teeth out
killed people over a fair amount of money
What could he possibly be afraid of?
death. revenge in hell.

So he happily traded the ability
to judge and think for himself
for the ability to sleep peacefully
at night

He needs a god
a god that kissed and hugs him
He needs a god
a god that gives him his blessing
He needs a god
a god to tell him what's right
          and what's wrong
He needs a god
a god to free him of his past sins
He needs a god
a god to make his soul live forever

the balls (if you don't read till end you'll think I'm an asshole but I'm actually a very sensitive poet)

2 beers ago
We were at the secret beach
(it is called secret beach)
Nobody but us
We swam out
Super far
Which takes balls
But different kind of balls

2 beers later
We're back at the magnificent hostel
(big pool, mowed lawn, stone steps, AC, big bedroom, giant bathrooms, clean beds, 5€ per night)
ALL alone
Below a starry sky
And I start touching and kissing
Her

Where did the balls come from?

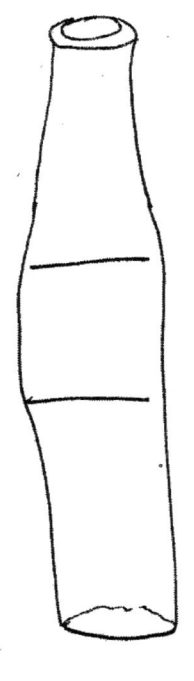

Beer for adults

After finishing business
I scootered to the canadian ladies
One had a cute face
The other was truly beautiful

Sometimes superficial good looking people
Are unbearably repugnant
Straight up disgusting like cockroaches

And then there are normal people
Whose genuine smile will ease your mind
Whose light laugh will lure you out of your shell
Whose movement through space and time
will make you forget yourself
For a moment

Emergency

A REAL POEM

ROSES ARE RED
YOUR LIPS ARE RED
SYMBOLIC HEARTS ARE RED

COULDN'T CARE
　ABOUT YOUR PERIOD

CAUSE I'M
　YOUR BLOODY IDIOT

the young germans

it all started with a simple question
she was standing next to her friends
they seemed close
almost like people in a realationship

She seemed so dull
She only was a flower
a fruit
just ready and juicy
just ready to pick

the tongues loosened
the cocktails, the cheap cocktails
                    helped
surrounded by talkative people
from boring travellers
to alluring weirdos
everybody was there

When the needed level was
                finally reached
We parted, went to something
        that one might even call
                    a club
I was lucky
Oh god was I lucky
But one is always lucky
when one feels good
without intentions

glances were biting my lips
eyes were undressing me
hands were touching my butt
    (that's sexual harassment)
people were shouting questions
        in my ear
me?
I was just vibing to the
    backstreet boys
and to sicko mode

Our friends left
they drank too much
couldn't handle their liquor
the young germans, huh?

shorty after they were gone
it seemed like a good time
to get the fuck away

back at the hostel
we went swimming in the pool
then we snuck into her dorm
because the lousy drunks
    annoyed her
and that's how I
    got kicked out of the hostel

back home

there's a girl back home
She loves me
But she has a boyfriend

She is a cat person
She herself is a cat
That's why she needs a dog

A good boy
who comes when his name is said
Who is devoured by guilt,
      when she gives him the guilty look
who follows her to the toilette
      when she stands up

Life would be easy as a good boy
But not very exciting

How can I tell she loves me?
It would take too long
It would take too long
I leave the explanations and descriptions
      to the scientists
And watch her bore herself to death
And leave the explanations and descriptions
to the scientists
till it goes *CLICK*

lone ranger in pseudo isolation

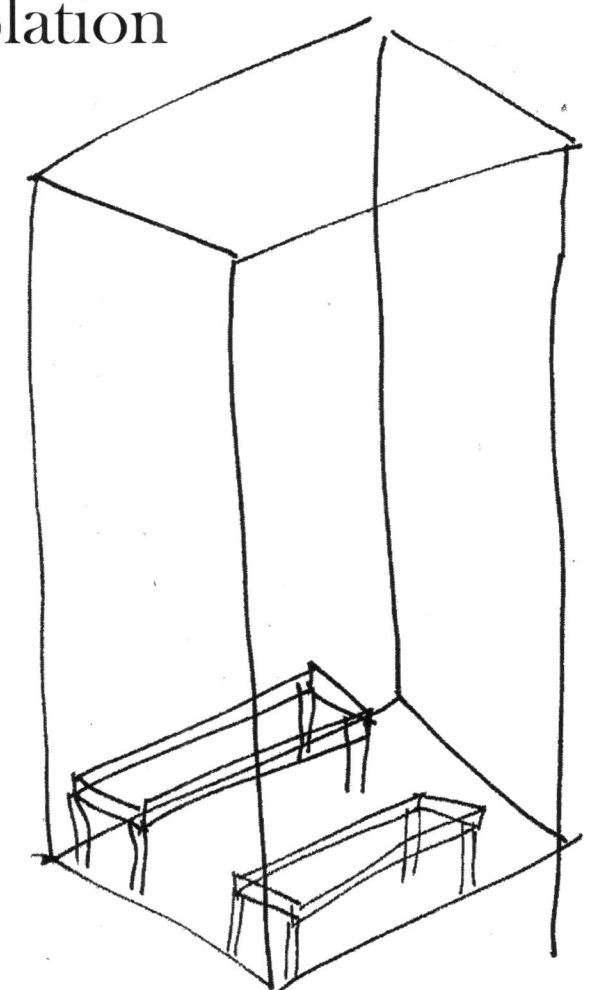

ISOLATION

SEX NEXT TO THE KITCHEN

I HEAR THEM FUCKING
MOANING
IT TICKLES IN MY BRAIN

TIME TO GET UP
KITCHEN, CEREAL
ASHTRAY ON THE TABLE
COLD SMOKE IN THE AIR

THE CREAKING STOPPED
DEAD SILENCE
CAN THEY HEAR
THE SPOON HITTING
THE BOWL?

I'D RATHER WALK IN
AND ASK IF I CAN
  JOIN

BUT I DON'T LIKE
THE GIRL

my wishlist for christmas

I wish I would have 7 lifes

One to marry my first love
One to make my parents proud
One to become a football player
One to become a drug addict/homeless
One to live like Charlie Sheen

but here I'm stuck with the
inevitable friction the scarcity
of time evokes

It's fine

One to learn everything about
                              history

basic bitch motivational quote/ig caption

Look around
Look at your phone
Every contact in your phone
      will be dead
And you too
100 years tops

Funny how we feel insecure
      not wanting to go out
           because of a pimple
                a hideous pimple

But it's easy to talk smart
      to talk of the future and time
           and meaningless life

All we ever have is the present
      so be insecure
           or not

when I'm at home

The door is open
The steps get louder,
            clearer

„Hello?" ← it is warm,
                  soft
there (in the doorway) stands
.....
A woman
MY woman

If I could only
posses her ....
Like a phone?

No, it would make it
worse.
No,
like a song
certainty is for
the weak

don't tell me
where you go baby

Just knock
Just come in

Damage limitation

The first time we met
I was kinda nervous
ready to go home
when my phone vibrated
smoking my cig slowly

You were more than
just nervous

Was it destiny?
A kind of fucked up
      revenge plotted by life?

You wanted to show me
that you're crazy
and spontaneous and a slut

it worked
we parted eventually
you were excited
really excited

I haven't seen you
like that
ever since

I had to play it cool
I always have to

But deep inside
I knew I was fucked
as I walked along
with my friend
away from you,
I felt the fire
heating up my blood,
explaining to him why I'm fucked

would've been perfect
but we can't let
our guard down
to reveal who we are
it has been too long
and too painful

When done

A guy, I know and have
the utmost respect for
stood in the sand
and screamed at the ocean
let it all out
then spat in the ocean
I was lying beside a pile of trash meanwhile
Twigs and coconuts (organic trash)

Later he told me about it and said:
That's it, I'm done with it.

You could call his act theatrical
but the fact
that he was in drama class
(And very talented)
And the fact that we had a head full of acid
legitimize his act

I think when
You're done you're done
No need for words
Or actions

days and days

You have me in the palm of your hand
With your eyes
With your walk
With your legs
Your soft skin

Well, this is
Superficial I think
And you have heard it
You've seen it
it is clear but
you still have to check
one more time
only one more time

maybe tomorrow it won't
be the same
who cares
about it?
You and I
maybe..........

Faking it

Some people have it
Some people don't
Some people try to earn it
but those lose their teeth
at night
in unlucky dreams

It lies in the air
You can see it in the fog
Some suck it in their lung
But it isn't the same
twice.
Impossible/Never

Nothing was ever found
on the outside
even the deaf and blind
knew that

three huge pillows
sleeping on my bed
spiders and silverfishes
are fighting over the toilet
Sometimes I can hear the neighbors
Finding it
in the middle of the night
but most times
I don't

The most dreadful creatures
About 50% among us
Truly found it once
And thought they can
put it on a leash
and walk it like a dog
Or even worse
they
just
fake
it

Edgy love poem

Lean and elegant
And the skin like silk
Who could restrain
Leave his hands in his pockets

It's like math
without the logical coherence
I told her something
And laughed
But it was a valid argument
It was how I felt

she laughs, she cries
the shadow of a bird
crosses my balcony
the flowers are satiated
with water
We met in the day
We should meet in the night
sometimes
I figure sometimes

silence

YOU COULD GO OUTSIDE
AND LOOK AT THE MOON
IN SILENCE

MAYBE THINK ABOUT
SOMETHING

NOTICE THAT YOU'RE
HOLDING ON
TO YOUR CIGARETTE
AND THE LIGHTER
IN YOUR POCKET

TAKE A PUFF
LOOK AT THE MOON
IN SILENCE

OR MAYBE
YOU COULD TAKE
A SHIT

simple dog doing tricks

And it was in there
I had a peek
and lost it
that's all I can remember

I woke up, naked
to a podcast
because of the cold
I sought refuge
        under the blanket
But they asked me
to do some tricks

So the show was on
They know
        I'd do about anything
            for breakfast
                in bed

edible

edible
edible
edible

my girl is all edible

she puts coco nut oil
on her tits
and some kind if butter
on her lips

she says
she's all about the sauce
the sauce
(has to be creamyyyy)

she asks
innocently
if it is too spicy

**IT CAN'T BE TOO SPICY
I SCREAM**

But it was a little too spicy

tinder covid simulation/roulette

WHEN I THINK OF HER
I FEEL LITTLE TO NOTHING
MAINTAINING A HEALTHY DISTANCE
LOSING IT IS TOO EASY
A MOMENT OF UNAWARENESS
    AND IT SLIPPED

THE MIRROR SHOWS ME
THE SCARS IN MY FACE
FROM ANOTHER PLACE

BUT WHEN I SEE HER
WITH HER STUPID SMILE
HER TILTED EYES
THE PERFECT TITS

I FALL, FROM UP HIGH
I FALL
    AGAIN

AND I WISH IT WOULD BE
 JUST HER BODY
BUT BEING SPOILED
WITH LOVELY MESSAGES
WITH LOVELY MASSAGES

IT IS TOO MUCH
I DIDN'T ASK FOR
   ALL THIS

FURTHERMORE
I HAVE NOTHING TO OFFER

BUT SHE THINKS
      THE SAME
SO WE'RE EVEN

Aliens

How could I be bored
With all the articles
About something that is going on

As I read more and more
About the plague (~1350)
The sky is clearing
Children are playing in the park
My phone is ringing
And I'm uncomfortable
Feeling the need to go out
And see people and have fun
When in my room there are
Seven lifetimes of work and work
And work that I love
And love and love (not real work)

As we speak about gorillas
And bears
And who would win the fight
A wild boar runs toward me
We are humans (intelligent)
The trick is to gouge its eyes out
But it was just a heavy breathing,
always last breath taking, pug
I push him away
with my ragged shoes
and look at the owner

As I find pleasure
In giving pleasure to others
I found myself
Talking about myself

Carole baskin killed her husband
We know that
She laughs
We are shocked
But secretly entertained
Eating popcorn

all we do is get fucked

All we do is
Get fucked
And fuck

I wonder if these
Things will ever change

But I've heard a 70 year old say
He thought about the same thing
When he was younger
And he's still thinking
About pussy all day

He said it doesn't stop
But it isn't of any importance

The real question is:
When you meet somebody
And the person gives you a fake smile
Do you appreciate the effort?
Or despise the phony?

Evolution

I can still here the birds
chirping from yesterday

And I already see the trees
      of tomorrow

But for now I am confused

      and I'm waiting
For nothing special
     just waiting
Because I have to let it go

Crows are testing the
twigs, in front of the
balcony

but went away

my phone vibrates
I turn in off
there is no time now

Revolution

Some people are so alone
they hold you hostage
with their genuine sadness

The world is a bad place
for too honest people
They are deemed weak
boring

humans need drama
we need friction
we dance around
leisurely trying
to net get caught

and it's all fun
and games

till you get hurt

A lost day

He had to choose
Noodles or Money?
After dialing
and hanging up
It was noodles
as yesterday
and the yesterday of yesterday

The water was boiling (boiling)
the water in his skin
The sun had burned him
and shining, it was shining

To make things worse
somebody shat with
the door open
The whole flat was
reeking of shit

good kids bad kids

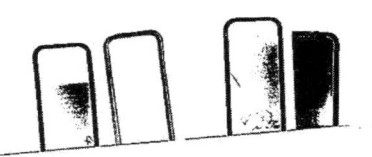

GOOD KIDS
MAKE BAD GROWN UPS

BAD KIDS
MAKE OBEDIENT ADULTS

FAITHFUL PEOPLE
ARE SNITCHES

AND THE WORLD
KEEPS SPINNING

VOLCANOS ERUPT

AND WE LIVE
IN A SOCIETY

THAT OPPOSES
NATURE

hotbox in a forest

it was a sober day
until things happened
the frogs croaked
it was a call
when they suddenly stopped
as if they wanted to hear
the conversation

in a dark forest
shone one light
the insides of a car
outside were random noises
inside it was similar

they were making noises
with their mouths
and blinking
with their eyes

the fog got dense
too dense to see
inside

Waiting for the train

We beat corona
Humanity won
We partied altogether
30 people

(my phone died)
It is easy to drink beer
It is easy to do another line
It is easy to talk a lotta shit
But

In the morning:
headache,
nausea

Train station
35 minutes delay
Paid 50 cents to take a shit
Vomiting was for free

Lied outside
On the pavement
In the sun
Hoping nobody would bother me
Waiting for the train

CRAVING

FROM TALKING
TO SMOKING
TO DRINKING
TO FUCKING
TO EATING
TO SMOKING
TO DRINKING
TO FUCKING
TO ~~THE END~~
SLEEPING
~~×~~ CALLING IT A DAY

it's time

Time to sin
Time to lie
Time to respond instantly
Time to give homeless people alcohol
Time to fuck anal
Time to take a cold shower
Time to stay sober
Time to smoke two cigarettes at once
Time to squash silverfishes with bare fingers
Time to look people in the face
Time to sleep without a pillow
Time to sleep without a blanket
Time to ridicule people for their believes
Time to cynically destroy your façade
Time to eat pizza for breakfast
Time to eat cereal with water
Time to scream
Time to really laugh
Time to argue with yourself in public
It's time to lose your mind
        and go 21st century crazy

the waitress

THE WAITRESS ASKED ME
WHAT I WANTED TO DRINK
I SAID WATER

WOW, YOU'RE SUCH A PLANT
SHE SAID

I WASN'T OFFENDED
I LIKE PLANTS
AND I LIKE WATER

riding bikes all day

when you get
the chance
you can take it
or let it take you

the words often
are not important
it's the mouth
don't mention tonality

push hard
go far
looking back
it's never that far

and if you don't
remember
you'll forget it

Letter_for_a_girl.mp3

Oh baby
I'm always drinking
when I'm with you
it isn't healthy
but the sex is good

But when you text me
I turn off my phone

Oh baby
I have some cute photos
of us
and sometimes

I think of you
and write something down

But I'm not a phone guy
don't take it personally

Fair play

TODAY WAS A GOOD DAY
I ATE CEREAL
HAD SEX WITH MY EX
MY FLATMATES LIGHTED
   THEIR FARTS
THERE ARE NO
      SILVER FISHES VISIBLE

BUT I LOST INCHESS
AND BLACKJACK

FAIR
PLAY

I was done and took a last puff

Dramatic
I hate it
say what you want
or make a compliment
No hot air in summer
My brain is melting
But the night
       makes me forget
But the night
       makes me take the lie
and embellish it
with all the true beauty
of opportunities
it, the lie, doesn't melt
but burns in the fire

human interaction

I was on my way
To a friend (to a party)

I got off the train
And waited at the semaphore
For the light
to turn green

It was dark, it was fresh
it was not raining

Beside me stood two girls
and some other people
waiting for the green light
As I glance over at them
I see her round ass fighting the leggings
Hard grappling
They looked too clean though (the girls)
(I can say in hindsight)

I wasn't even drunk
Just full of myself

I said: "Hey,
What are you up to tonight?"
(with a sly grin)

The first reaction was none at all
Then, after a moment or so,
the pretty one
Slowly turned away from me
With her whole body

That was the worst reaction a human being
Could obtain
But it's still better then lying in bed
Asking yourself
"WHAT IF????????"

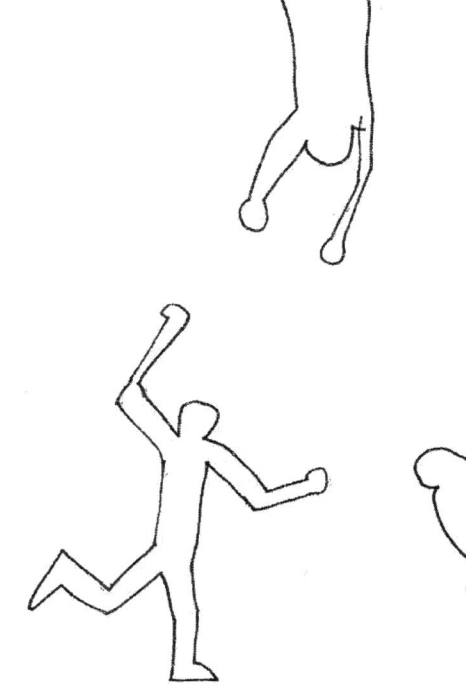

beauty and perfection

SOMETIMES
LIFE IS SO PERFECT
YOU WANNA CAPTURE
THE MOMENT
LIKE A PICTURE
AND LOOK AT IT
FOREVER

SOMETIMES
LIFE IS SO BEAUTIFUL
YOU JUST WANNA
KILL YOURSELF

A VAGUE LOVE POEM

YELLOW
MELLOW
PILLOW
SPOONING
SICK
AND HAPPY

BRIGHT
NIGHTS
SMOKE
TEARS
LICKING
KISSING
KISSING

Sometimes hate

Sometimes i get frustrated
Sometimes i walk around and there is
Nothing good
Nothing that makes sense
Nothing that adds value to the world
People walking around
With their cloths
And their believes
Openly displayed
And I hate them

Sometimes
As I walk past
200 year buildings
I see the labour
The work
The fear
That made them do this
And I see
It is necessary
They needed to be pushed
I talk to my father and hear
That it is necessary
They needed to be forced
They liked it

Sometimes when I walk through
Karlsplatz
And stop in front of the church
And just enjoy it
Enjoy my existence
Look up in awe

A businessman in his suit
Would catch my attention
And I'd like to drop 2 drops
Of acid in his coffee
To make him see it
To make him lose his mind
And I see a woman fully covered
Fully covered in clothes
Because her husband forced her
And his father forced him
And I really feel the urge
To rip off that stupid clothing
And make her the way she was born
Let the sun shine on the skin
Make her head free
For the first time
Before mine gets cut off

Tomato titty

At times
I think
I always knew
I'd be me

But that's a
Lie (*lie*)

Because nobody is born
With the ability to think
Hence my personality
Is borrowed (*borrowed*)
From the abstraction of language

The more I think
"I am me"
The tighter the chains get

Two ways to win an argument

1) Realize that you selfworth is not dependant on the outcome of the argument

2) Raise your voice

fomo

Then I cried
because I thought
about bad things
which were beautiful
situations
in which I wasn't
involved

But it wasn't that
        serious

Just a moment
of weakness

chaotic arrangement of words

Somebody needed numbers
But the slaves
knew their power
But they felt pity

In a room with windows
the pane cold be
A painting
If you let it be

And the pain is a
part of your being
and the present

and I allowed it
that's nice
sun, sun, sun, sun

Whatsapp poem

this night i dreamt
of your lips
they were slightly opened
like a flourishing rose

i kissed your lips
full of passion
as they were devoted
to myself

i wanted to pluck it
your rose
awakened only
when the pain
of the thorns
busted my fingers
like a balloon

summer sweat

Dirty dancing

A girl glanced at me
Only for an instant I noticed
The glare in her eyes
Then she
Walked backwards
And pressed her butt against my
Guts

shooketh
I was absolutely disgusted

"is this all you can offer?
You ought to strike up a conversation
Or introduce yourself first
Ask me about my name"

But it was too late
It was too late

Toxic masculinity

I said to her:
„Bro I piss so hard,
Last time
I destroyed the toilette
The piss cut right through
the china toilette
Like a laser beam"

And everybody laughed
Because it was a joke

inside

I could slice
somebody open
like an apple

and still
I wouldn't know
what's inside them

and I think that's
beautiful

too dumb to suffer

Luckily
I'm too dumb
To suffer seriously
Because at some point
When I've suffered enough
In my opinion at least
I'll be tired of suffering
And will forget it
Or forget myself
It doesn't matter
As long as it works

blue hair pink pill

The girl with the
blue hair
made me snort the
pink pill

For a moment
I asked myself
if it was a
real orgasm

But whom could
I trust
if not myself
and my perception?

Nervous

Think about the last time
you were nervous

Were you with a woman
on the couch?
high as shit?

Weren't you both hoping
that you'd make a move?

Wasn't your heart pounding?
didn't you think for a
moment she'd see it
through your shirt?

Weren't you thinking
about the move?
picturing it in your head?
but she was too far
        she was too close
                too real
Your arm became rock solid
and too heavy to lift

SUNDAY

SUN
HEAT
SKIN
SWEAT
GRASS
WATER
FISHES
TEK
TENSION
TITS
NOT SEEING MY FEET
IN THE WATER
BECAUSE IT IS
   TOO DIRTY
GETTING HIGH
GETTING NAKED
DROWNING IN CLOUDS

roundabout

she went around
      and around

I went around
      and around

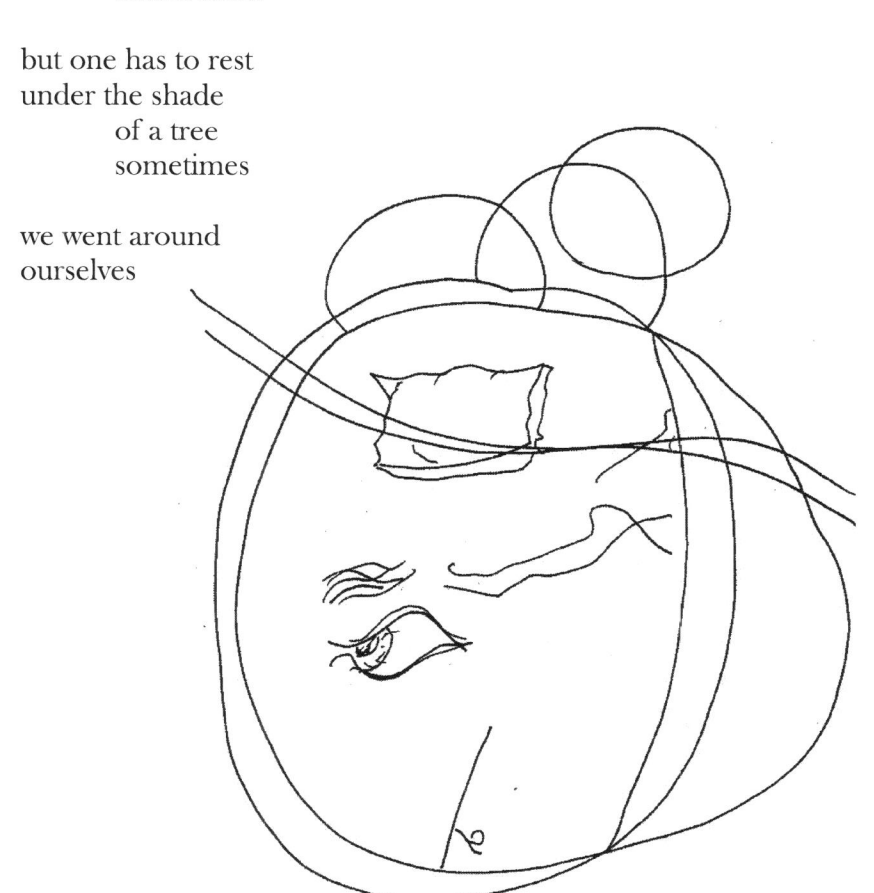

but one has to rest
under the shade
      of a tree
         sometimes

we went around
ourselves

Pussy juice

At night
when it's dark
I turn on the light
to see the blood
to see the action
      and the pain

because the morning
makes us forget

At day
the sun was up
and I looked straight
                at it
But don't worry
I was blind before
and I saved some
      of your pussy juice
to pour it over my eyes

deserted

the winds shifted
I only could wait
wait in the desert
and play with my pubic hair

I thought I had moved
When the wind
blew the sand mountains
incessantly
away

My world was small now
But I found an oasis
(accidently)
With dates and palms
But I didn't like the music
So I laid naked in the sand
in the sun
In order to evaporate

Life hack 1

If you feel too dependent
on one person

just split your dependency
among many people

that way you will feel
way freer
(more free)

Low end real as fuck shit

soft skin
at the end of my fingers
soft like
a volleyball floating in
dead water

symphonic smell
at the end of the bed
symphonic like
cherry blossoms with notes of
drain cleaner

a fleshy pink
on sky blue background
by a cloudy wall, white

disharmony
equilibrates itself
in motion
(I was gravity)

the sun made me soft

music came from the kitchen
it sounded like chinking of forks
the sun had made me soft
soft like high like oily water in the danube
I thought about all the women I don't wanna
have sexual intercourse with
"anti-objectification"

music came from the other side of the danube
we were walking along the bridge
it was a long walk
it was a long bridge
MAD vibes, mad
the crazy guy with the black eye looked at me manically
I lost the staring contest (first loss since 2006)
he had a black mohawk
he gave our black dog some black back rubs
I didn't feel like dancing
so I watched him giving the dog back rubs
hoping to start another staring contest

SUDDENLY, suddenly
a sudden wave of SOMETHING
hit me straight between my eyes
went through me hips into my legs and up to my shoulders
my arms were floating in the air like in water
we started screaming and shuffling and mocking people
to feel better about ourselves
to distance ourselves from ourselves
to be free
(mocking people with the typical dance moves
people do
when they don't dance but just make the moves everybody
does
the moves the whole scene does to a special type of music
because that's just what they do)

yes I felt very good and very special
and god didn't help me
I did it all by myself (sober)

foreplay

contrary to common beliefs
foreplay
doesn't start in bed

it starts outside
where you perceive yourself in third person
with the first glance
the first steps
towards each other

every word
ignited by the unsatiated desire
heavy and lofty at the same time
morbidly sordid and swift
every syllable
red and striking

but the most important
THE MOST IMPORTANT
is the silence
to express the inexpressible
(as in classic music)

To burn and burn and burn
Make it last years and decades!!!!!!!!

(it's about *the* lust
not *the* satisfaction)

Salty but sweet liquid

I wish you would know me better
but as long as I can play your guitar
like santana, like gg allin
there are other things to worry about

You walk around like a cat
shamelessly purring
and I hope you have 7 lifes
because you are wasting a couple
with your nicotine addiction
and the other shit

I put my coke in your straw
you put your piercings in my nipples
you saw my asshole
you saw me being an asshole

Fear of the future
spoils the present
only solution
is to plunge in head first

(but my dad once told me that one of his friends is now
paralyzed because he jumped head first into shallow water)

silver fish metaphor

It is quite a metaphor
That in our flat
We (or rather I)
Have a problem with silverfishes

Silverfishes are useful
They only appear
Where it is dusty
And moist
And they eat away the dust
And drink away the moistness

It was only when I saw
A big one
I'm talking <u>1 cm (0.4 inch)</u>
I ripped off toilet paper
Two sheets to be safe
Then tried to grab it
But it didn't work
Cause it was fighting back
It was really stressed/stressing me out
Until I pulled its fucking skin off
UNINTENTIONALLY

Under the skin
It was just white
Fucking pathetic piece of
Insect
Skinned by a pathetic human being

I asked myself
WHY
But it is a metaphor

extra soberness

Linking up the soberness
with good old travesty
in jesus own vagina
to lick the puddle
and kick the thirsty dog
in his non existent balls

flying into an butterfly
angrily (road rage) telling him
to „fuck off cunt"
before you noticed his sheriff's star
and you try to reconcile him
with your words (the words you just said to him)
(they were just words)
(but they evoked hostile feelings in the butterfly)
You cannot soften him
You're going to jail

nutting in the toilette
of a chic café
thinking of something absurd
thinking of how the you'd rape
someone who raped someone
because you have this weird fetish
being a sadist
with a well developed sense of justice

A picture

What's the point of being
sober
If you don't brag with
      your willpower?

What's the point of being
cool
If you're not constantly
      hinting at it?

What's the point of being
in love
If you don't tell everybody?

What's the point of being
happy
If the other don't know
how much you're enjoying
      your life?

A starry night

Just as I slid
in an orange dream
half awake, half surfing
I noticed I was alone
in my room

I realized I was alone
in my body

The wave caught me
pulled me underwater
I wasn't even the idea
of myself anymore
Not even the idea I think
others have of me

I was a drop in the
ocean

Then it was day
again

A DAY

I WOKE UP
LIED IN BED
JACKED OFF
WORKED OUT
ATE CEREAL
READ
WENT SWIMMING
WITH REAL FRIENDS
PLAYED MARIO KART
TOOK KRATOM

IT WAS SO ORDINARY
IT WAS PERFECT

Highest highs Lowest lows

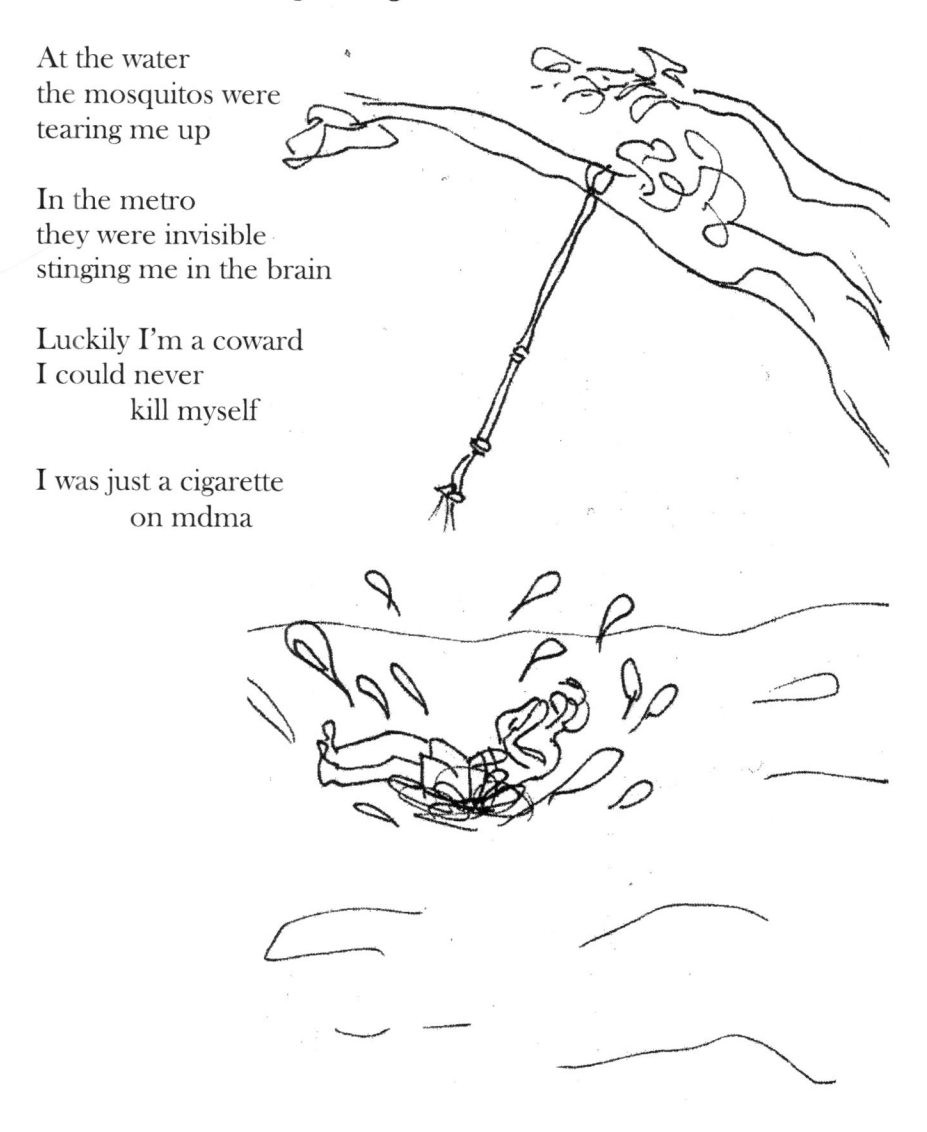

At the water
the mosquitos were
tearing me up

In the metro
they were invisible
stinging me in the brain

Luckily I'm a coward
I could never
       kill myself

I was just a cigarette
      on mdma

Life hack 2

Randomly check
your facial expression
to find out how you
really feel

the belly button

I nearly didn't notice how time was passing
Because I had to ignore it
For my plan to make sense
And therefore
It was passing
Very fast

I told her
to kiss my bellybutton
Kiss my bellybutton
Why? Was the question
Just because
Was the answer
Then she kissed my bellybutton

Sie kissed it very sensually
It was as if
She was pushing
With her endearing kiss
The blood
Up my dick

I've never did anything
Alike
She said
Me neither
Said I
Then I climbed
Out
Through the window

DESINFECTION

YESTERDAY I BORROWED
FEELINGS FROM TOMORROW

TODAY WAS THE PRESENT
TODAY WAS THE DAY
SO I DID NOTHING

IF FEELINGS ARE
A BURNING FLAME
ONLY ASHES WILL BE LEFT

STERILE — (ANTI-BACTERIAL)
NOTHINGNESS AFTER PASSION

Last time i painted

I was on Ketamine
I haven't painted since
Because it feels like spoiling a dream
By talking about it
And reducing the sensations to words

I was in a bathtub
But instead of me rocking the water
Back and forth
The water rocked me
And soon I couldn't tell the brush from the paper
Or the air from the wall
The room swayed
With some weird jazz in the background
Melting my head

It wasn't until I was finished
(the world still a two dimensional canvas)
I noticed that my center of gravity
Lied a few meters behind me
And was swiftly drawing circles in the kitchen

The legends

The night started out yellow
As yellow as eggyolk
And as innocent as breakfast

Under supervision
The jokes were kept impersonal
The drinks were kept at an arms length

As soon as the guest slammed the door
The white of the eyes
Mirrored the sordid thoughts
The barrier of societal expectations/notions
          (as friend groups and pride)
Shattered right there
Under the glistening rain of white crystals

The nose burned
The brain burned
The heart burned
The crotch burned
And it all burned down
Before they could make it
Out

In the morning
Not quite as innocent as the
Beginning of the night
The legends were laughing
And laughing
And laughing
And drinking beer at 9 am
And laughing like no one could ever laugh

fear of commitment

Who would've thought
that fear of commitment
doesn't come from the tireless cry
for freedom
but the fear of opening
oneself
getting intimate and eventually
getting hurt?

Why I love whores

because they always genuinely whore around
in the moment

and thus it becomes
overwhelmingly real

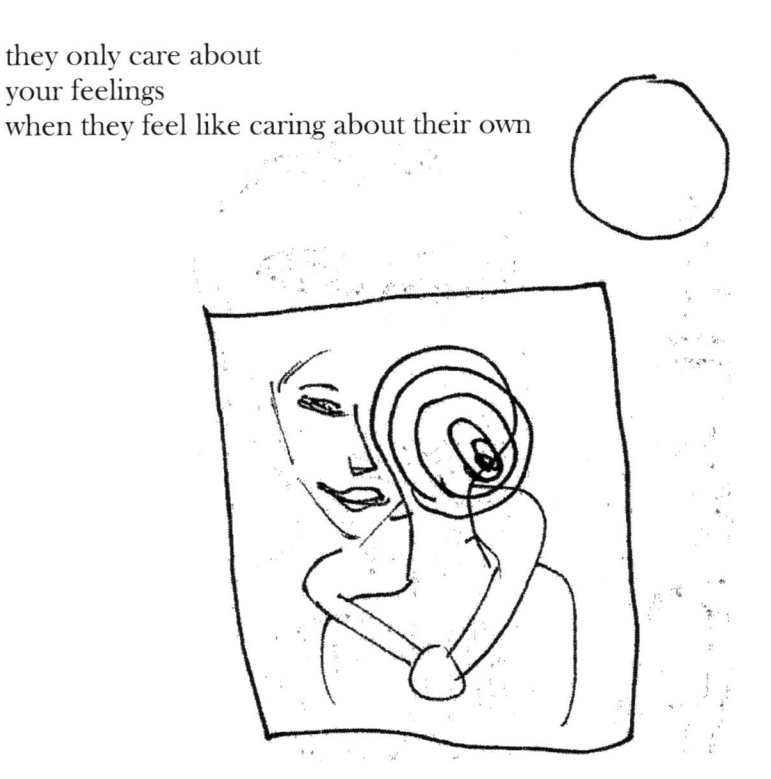

they only care about
your feelings
when they feel like caring about their own

PEAKING

LYING IN THE SUN
~~CLOSING~~ EYES CLOSED
SUNLIGHT
ETERNAL CONSCIOUSNESS

ONLY THE FLY
TICKLING MY ELBOW
~~SHOWS~~ ME THE LIMIT
OF MY BEING

Identity

Having plans is good
Having something to be
happy about
The idea of the future

Having plans to visit
someone
Being a stranger
Having only your face
Giving your face
       a persona

Gathering all possibilities
of freedom of action
In your face
In a new country
In a new city
In new words

New presence in the present

Preach

It's funny how you discuss
sex at noon
and that sex needs intimacy

and that it needs emotions

that it is the incarnation
of the metaphysical love

that sex nowadays is
dehumanized

It's just about fucking
and how disgusting that is

and at night you just
get fucked up
and end up having
wild impersonal
stranger sex

DIGNITY

I WAS MOVING
LIKE A FLEA-RIDDEN
DOG
BETWEEN THE SHEETS

SHE WAS HISSING
LIKE A SNAKE
AND HOWLING
LIKE A COW

THE SPECTATORS
WERE ENTERTAINED

THEN WE LEFT THE BED
THE BATTLEFIELD
LIKE THE UPRIGHT WALKING
HUMANS WE ARE

BLIND!!!!!!!!!

If someone would ask
me: Why are you constantly
trying to have sex?

I would answer:
Because I was ugly
and now I gotta make
good use of my life
to show appreciation

But really it's pathetic

Sex is being sold
since they started
mass producing condoms
in 1870 and I'm just
a victim of the
industry

Smalltalk

If you find yourself
in a seduction
not ridden by routine
start counting
because people get
romantic about the
pain the seduction
inflicted

but without pain
the idea wouldn't cost
              enough
would never be flesh

to untangle yourself
you have to highlight
the bad traits of your
object of seduction
like you did with the ideas
of you two being together
to make it even

Pesto-Pasta

I met an angel
so beautiful and light
so sensitive and fragile
shining, glowing

I didn't dare to look
her in the eye
I was afraid to break her
with an inadvertent
         manic glance

The only time the first sign
of wrinkles appeared on
her divine face
was when she talked about
her ex-flat mate who was
a soft cuddly teddy bear
but started doing bdsm-shit
and beating up women

Playing scrabble in the garden and drinking liquor

A JUDGEMENT SAYS EVERYTHING ABOUT THE JUDGER

AND NOTHING ABOUT THE PERSON/THING BEING JUDGED

schönheit

Yes baby do the
        dirty trick
One more
never the last time
Although I learned
        my lesson
            the last time
And I swear
        I would play
            again
If you did it
        with grace

When talking becomes redundant

When something
is truly beautiful

Why would you
interrupt your
perception
by action

instead of
enjoying it?

Steady simpin'

Sometimes I think about the girl
Whose fridge broke down
therefore she only ate toast bread
with toast cheese
(because these processed cheese slices
don't need to be stored in a fridge)

the girl with the exquisite
but slightly shrewd face
with a streak of malice
and the body made out of
flesh
dotted with birthmarks

whose rent was due
three months due
therefore she only ate toast bread
with toast cheese
sometimes cucumber

the girl who was lighting
cigarette after cigarette
when we weren't
busy

whose shower broke down
then she
came
to my place
to shower

sometimes I think about her
and ask myself
how much longer
will she last?

Friction

Sitting, smoking
The mad man was laughing
giggling, leaned forward
grinning into himself
and interrupted me
to talk about the ego
that it's not necessary

I let him finish
(I already knew my argument)
watched his fingers cramp
counted the seconds
counted myself counting the
                      seconds
As he repeated himself
suddenly I heard a
Big bang, like a whistle

All became tragically
                  comical
and I was free

The mirror

IF YOU LOOK LONG ENOUGH
INTO THE MIRROR

YOU WILL NOTICE THAT
IT'S ONLY A SURFACE

AND THAT IT'S DIRTY
AND THAT YOU SHOULD
CLEAN IT

Frog shit

In another life
This all would make sense
And we'd be looking at the sky
and see somebody guarding over us
and every misfortune would make sense
and every blessing would be a gift
and we wouldn't be so greedy
and ask for more all the time

In another life
I would be a frog
Having some amphibian thoughts
About the water and the eggs
Eating flies
Eating the flies that couldn't find
The shit (which they love)
The cycle would be complete
By me turning them into frog shit

internalization

Like an apple
I would like to eat you
then you would be
a part of me
and I would guard
  you
with my body
not knowing
not sensing
that the stomachacid
is dissipating you

working long happy hours

Today
as I came home drunk
I laid down on the couch
and made myself sad
because this inhuman joy
soon would've torn
my mind apart

I only noticed
as I was lying there
that I can't sense
the feelings from others
anymore
that I can't distinguish
anything anymore

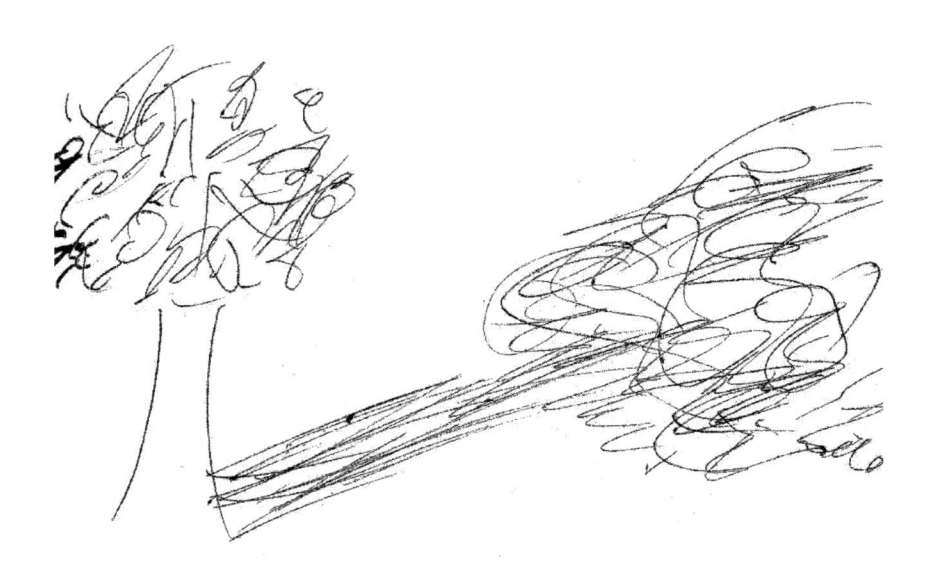

Conversation with god

Last Night
I spoke to god, no
God spoke to me

I was laying naked on
my bed, jacking off, with
the neighbors trying to avert
their glances from me, smoking
their cigarettes on the balcony

Thus he spoke:
"You stupid piece of shit
if you believe your wrongdoing
every molecule in your flesh will
project it outside and every other molecule
outside of your poor organism you call body
will perceive this emotion (e:nergy in motion)
and thus have the justification to
burn you down with your
own imaginary guilt

Trembling I jizzed in my sock
and hauled it in the bin

Love <3

When I think about love
it might be something as
easy as the blue sky
a blue sky with a little
cloud
or two
but simple
something the eye can't grasp
too vast
too far
too blue

only if you keep looking
at the blue sky
where you can't really
see anything
you might notice
the blue sky slowly and softly
enveloping you, looking back at you
                            PERVADING YOU
being everywhere... (meanwhile you lost the idea of your
body)
and making you
crazy
losing your shitttt
Now all you can think of is the strawberry
yoghurt from elementary school

Party Paradox

People who get fucked up every week
Think they're breaking the routine
Letting lose and letting go
When their behaviour is really some neurosis
Which impels them to delete their hard disk
Which blocks out congruent and coherent
thoughts
Keeps them save in their hole of delusion
Keeps them sound in superficial relationships
Everybody has the same plan

uncanny observations

people can be sad
but when they start to suffer in their imagination
and feel pity for themselves
they get depressed
depression = self-pity (at least in the beginning)
depression is like opening the fridge for the
third time even though you know there's
nothing you wanna eat
(buying new food would be leaving your comfort zone)

people like to get complimented for their talents
because they think that is the way they are (natural state)
and their inherent talents represent their being the most
that's why people secretly take pride in their mental issues
because that's their way of dealing/coping with life
therefore natural
and a true part of themselves
(it's the same reason why
I'd rather like to get a compliment on my dick
than on my intellect)

realization of my last acid trip

How can something be
inconvenient?

Only if you judge it
and compare it
to something you
learned to like
it becomes inconvenient

If you shower with
cold water and just
feel the cold
instead of fighting
it, it becomes
wonderful

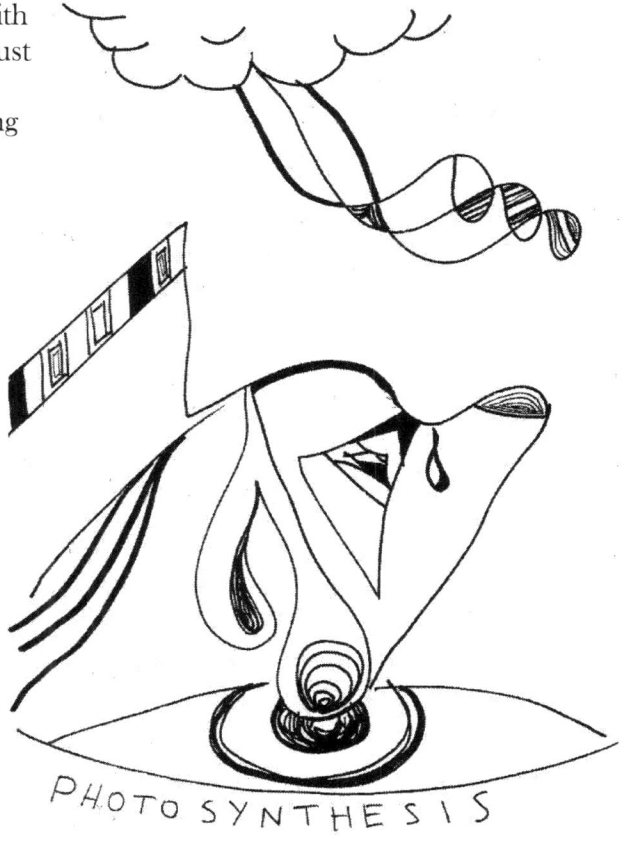

PHOTOSYNTHESIS

irresponsibility and heartbreak

They say driving drunk is irresponsible
Because you could kill someone
But are you going to freeze to death?

They say dying is irresponsible
Because it is not you who suffers
But your family and friends

Don't tell me anything about heartbreak
Today I saw my tindermatch
Hand in hand with a boy

Waves of sobering intoxication

In a strange night
we walked towards
      the future
and her pretty face
was the lantern
and her crazy eyes
were the light

With every word that fell
between us
I enjoyed her more
With every sip of wine
I got drunker
and she got uglier
but I liked her better this way

I was afraid to drink up
cus that would be
the end of the dream

painting date

It's awkward
when you call somebody
over
to paint
and then you really
end up painting
While the cool chick
who told you she gets
coke for free
just looks at her phone
and hears you
making funny noises
pouring yourself
into the canvas

Why you should pee with an open door

1) toilets are normally very small
   (so you have more space and feel relaxed)

2) to assert dominance
   (being not afraid to pee in front of others
   shows high levels of confidence)

3) to share this intimate moment
   and bond with someone you love

on the court playing

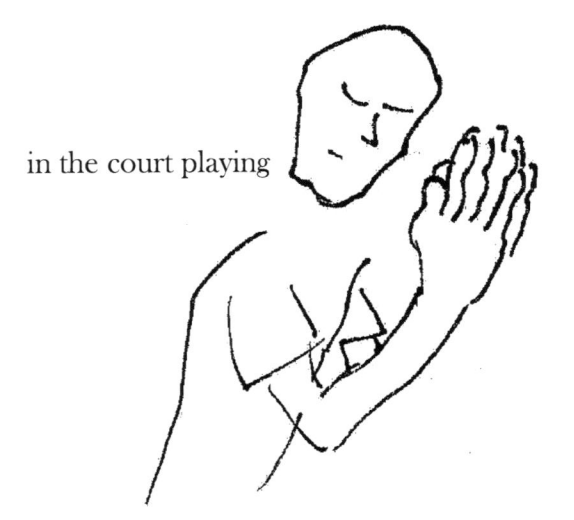

in the court playing

the fall

nipple fever

I curiously glance at the
      nipples
and they split
      my head
           in two

My hands were
      throbbing

The blood was
      stuck in
           my body

And I passed
      out
smelling
those fine
brown nipples

in my hand
      they melted
           to pure mdma

I didn't wash the
T-shirt
that guarded the
nipples
for a short period of time
for 1 week

It still bears the
      magic scent
when I hold it
to my nose
      I start

to sweat
and to tremble
the fever is
burning my
brain

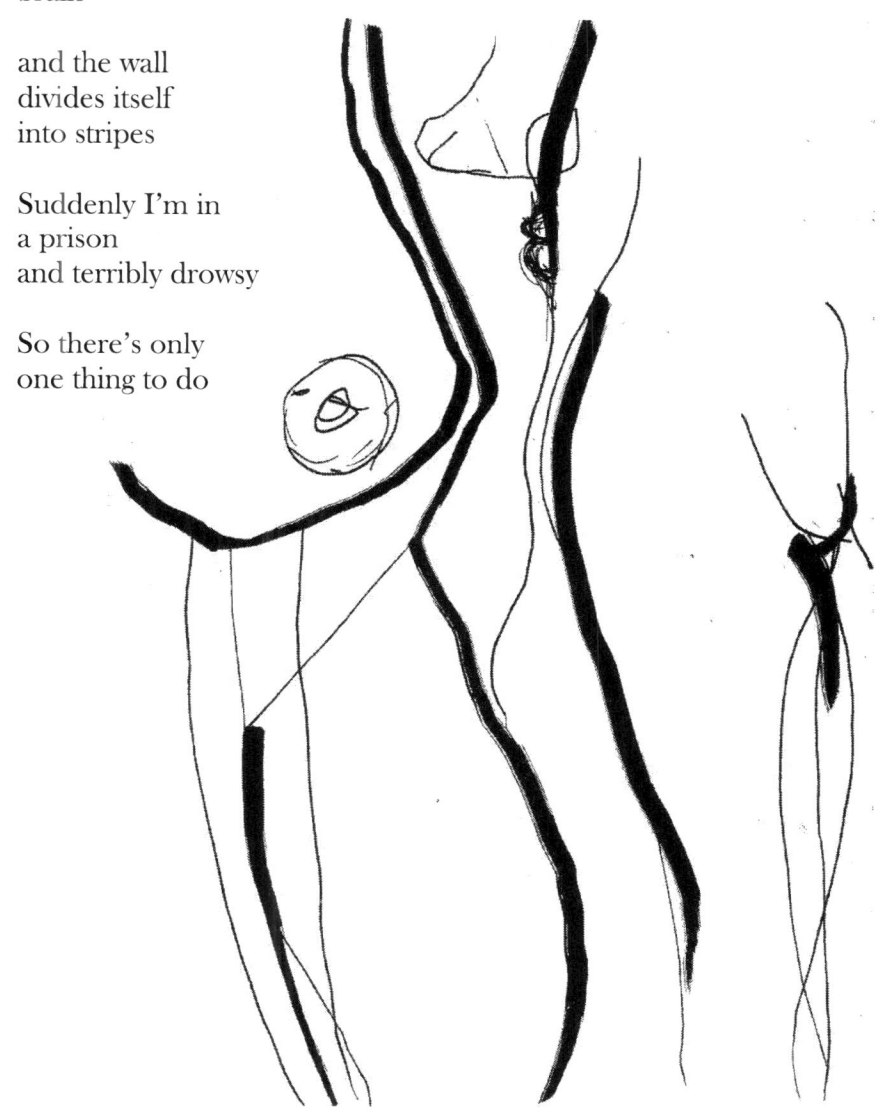

and the wall
divides itself
into stripes

Suddenly I'm in
a prison
and terribly drowsy

So there's only
one thing to do

omw to the metro

Condoms are whack
Police crossed a red light
At the station (metro)
junkies are smoking
Mixed feelings

I slept with a naked girl
Dreamed of girls with
         clothes on
Woke up
suddenly it wasn't enough

A good-looking old homeless
woman asked me for
money with a bag in
her hand
I was on ketamine and
reached in my pocket
    it was destiny

philosophy of quality

That there are people who count their sex partners is the perfect example to see how deeply shortsighted capitalism has influenced our way of thinking and values

Of course quality can only be reached through quantity but once you reach a certain level of quality the only goal can be to quantify quality and disregard quantity itself

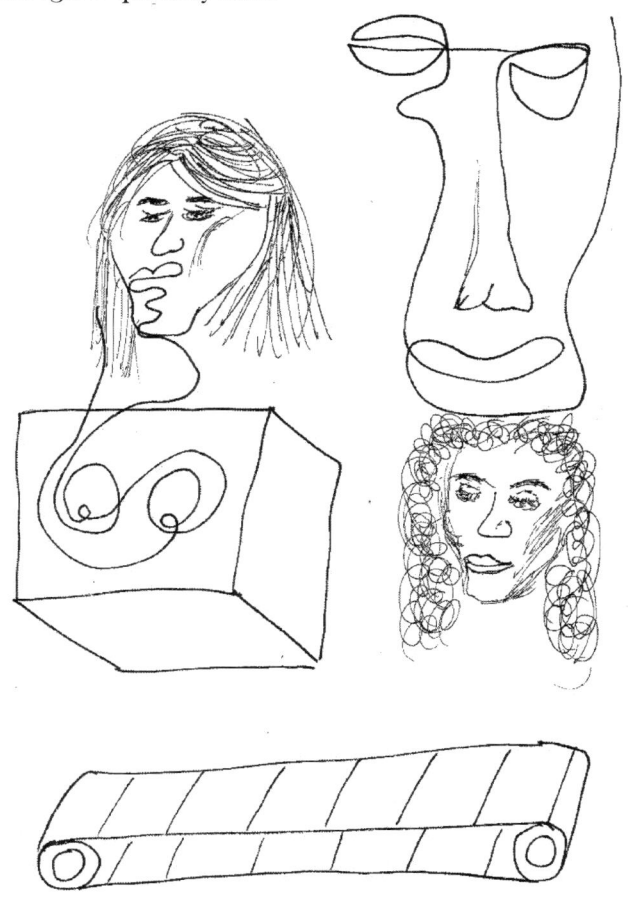

Thanks mother nature

> THANKS MOTHER NATURE
> FOR PUTTING OUR GENITALS
> BETWEEN OUR LEGS
>
> SO WE CAN KISS
> WHILE WE MAKE LOVE
> HAVE SEX
>
> ♡

perspective

HOW YOU VIEW YOURSELF MAINLY DEPENDS ON HOW YOU VIEW OTHERS

NOT HOW OTHERS VIEW YOU

Modern romance

She asked me „are you free tomorrow"
and I said „yes but you know that I either
have to decline directly or cancel it
tomorrow right before we'd meet
and then you have to do the same,
we have to go through this process at least twice
before we can meet in person again,
so that both parties know that each of
us has a very busy and interesting life
where we just can't make time for things
that come so suddenly and are so random
although we got along well last time and I'm
genuinly interested in getting to know you
or rather getting to know a new side of
myself through our relationship,
after all that we can mistake this already
invested time and energy for the
emotional connection that we otherwise
wouldn't have developed because we
lack the social skills but especially because
we are missing the guts to just give someone
our trust and just go with the flow because it
would be terrifying to think of some real
moments where we'd have to really think and
feel and act intuitively to arouse natural
sexual tension and then eventually we
can sleep with each other with an uneasy air of
hate but passionate hate and at last
call it complicated but complicated love"

short precarious glance

I don't want to tire
my face
So I turn my feelings
off

Shhhh.......
My forehead and my
cheeks .... are sleeping

You might scare them
and provoke a
         short-circuit
My eyes are resting
         on the ceiling
and I'm ignoring
all the people
in the lecture hall

Although I can feel
her glance
biting my skin
piercing my skin
ripping my skin

I can feel that
I'm involuntarily
drowing in her
thoughts
XXXXXXXXXXXXOOOO
I stretch............
The white of the eyes
is just too much

dans la provence

we went past her granny's house
which was ok, kinda
old
to her parents gigantic
villa

I couldn't articulate my
admiration for that
noble
piece of interior architecture
properly
and ended every sentence
with „yo"
(e.g: what a fat kitchen, *yo*!)

there was an electric bin
there was a touch screen oven
there was a fitness room
there was a sauna
and an infra red cabin
there was a stoopid huge pool
there was a winter garden
and a jacuzzi
on the first floor

and there were drops of period
blood
blood red period blood
on the wood floor
on the first floor
from me waggling my dick
to the bathroom
which (in my opinion)
gave this extraordinary
depiction of sterile
wealth
some profusely needed
character

when the dog chased its tail

in the instant
as the dog caught its tail
he became, so to speak, invisible
he dissolved
he solved his existence and his problem

when the woman with shoes
put her foot on the carpet
I realized she had boots on
and I heard the dirt
the filth
from the urinated streets
trampling down
the fabric
like crunchy autumn leaves

it was deeply worked into the matter

the color

after 3 glasses of wine
I was extraordinarily
exceptionally drunk
My brain was already stripping its clothes
off
we stood in front of the red café
to smoke a cigarette
(I was smoking and she was
watching me suck on the cigarette)

her eyes were voluptuously screaming
for a kiss
(a kiss)
and I asked her „why are you looking like
you want a kiss?"
she vividly denied: „no, no, no, ..." with hectic body
language
I continued in the confidential and calm voice:
„here prevail unwritten rules, didn't you know?
people don't kiss in this café, they put on a
mask and try to lift the mask of each
other, but this game is still ungraspably
intimate, because you choose
your own mask."

Degeneration

The door was still open
She gave me my things
and we both waited
for me to invite her in
The pressure mounted
and we moved in slow
motion
to not feel time so
terrible intense
on our skin
And then
she made a slight
movement towards
the door, to go
outside ....
And I shot it out:

„You wanna have a
look at the new flat?"
and we smoked
cigarettes
in my crooked room

The first puff
was so delicion
I took a bite of the cigarette
Her nipple piercings
looked so pretentious
through her shirt
I took a bite of
the nipples

And we talked
as if we were good
friends
without any intentions
But we drank gin
and did mdma
We lied in bed
I was a mushy piece
of loving and craving
confusion

She suddenly said:
„I have a boyfriend,
kinda."
I couldn't grasp the
meaning of these
words

So I slid my hand
in her pants
only to realize
that she was shaved
(??????????????)

Then came some
penis-in-vagina-action

My dick exploded
My heart exploded
and I died
for a short period
of time

After some more
and some more
mdma and tek
we were ready
to shape the stars
and she brought
the K to me in bed

it was like breakfast
in bed
But it was Ketamine
at night

My body ceased
to be flesh
and turned into a sensation

we didn't brush
our teeth
        that night

decent humans

OK, let's say
we don't want that
fast life trash
anymore
all the cheap and
replaceable products
like couches and
employees and
partners ....

What are the oprtions?
Behave like decent
human beings
and think about tomorrow?

The contrary of foreplay

I love that nasty shit
but when someone tries
to „subtly" squeeze her
tits into the camera
and sends it on
snapchat

I feel deceived
and disgusted
by that uncomely
behaviour

But most of all
I feel objectified
as a man-dog
which can be tamed
by some meat

giving love/preserving love

YOU GOTTA GIVE
  YOUR LOVE
   TO SOMEBODY ANYWAY

DON'T BE SO GREEDY
WAITING FOR THE
  "RIGHT ONE"

MAKE SOMEONE
   THE RIGHT ONE

LOVE DOESN'T GET
GREATER OR SPECIAL
 BY SAVING IT

Fingering with tobacco fingers

sleepy girl
having a distinct
unearthly smell

like a soapy rose
making love to
a mellow machine gun

small hands
with delicate fingers
and a shrill laugh
like radiator
and a heart
like
mowed lawn in summer

Nakedness
Nude
Penis
Eyes on Penis
Penis not for eyes
Shame?
Inconvenience
Fear
Like from a ghost
when one is younger
Guilt
No guilt found
only consolation
genuinly laughing
it off

brahman way of creating

When I shit on a paper
I grab a stick
And spread the shit
like butter on the paper
because otherwise worms would be bred
and would die
when no more shit remains

Practise

To practise patience
I fill my water bottle
with a slow stream
scarcely more than drops

To practise my memory
I learn 10 digits
of π every day

To practise dying
I meditate

To practise acting
I come up with
elaborate lies

To practise sex
I jerk off
6 times a day

To practise honesty
I imagine
myself without
a face

To practise life
I think of death

an abstract end

Unprecedented sympathy and remorse

It was only after
the second line of mdma
when I realized
no drug would get me as high
as I wanted to be
(as I needed to be)
But still was pushing for
another one

I realized
as we spooned
in bed
as I rubbed my pre-cum
on her back
and spread the water between
her thighs
on her ass cheeks
why my little kisses
tasted like sweet malignant cancer

there was a boyfriend
waiting somewhere
making everybody miserable

In summer

I was invited to a pool party
Indirectly
We went there
But i had forgotten my swim shorts
The only thing one needs for a pool party
But we had mushrooms with us
So we ate some mushrooms
my best friend and me

Somewhat later
We sat on the grass
8 or 10 people
And a girl started telling a story
In which she and a friend (who was present)
Went to the cinema
But her friend got stung by something
Before the film even started
And her foot swelled
And swelled
And got bigger and bigger
To the point where she had to take off her shoe

And i couldn't stop laughing
It wouldn't make any sense
I couldn't open my eyes
Hot tears of psychedelic retardation
running down my cheeks

And after i thought
I had made enough of an ass of myself
Amidst strangers
I jumped in the pool
Held my breath
Underwater
Watching the writhing surface
Draw dancing lines of light
On the turquoise bottom

window

I saw my
vis-a-vis neighbor
naked
stark naked
all of her breast
all of her hair
it was all there
a lovely sight
in a mild night
she shared the real
easy beauty
with the world
turned the pane into
a canvas
and i couldn't stop
looking
drooling like a 6-year-old

now i understand why
my upper
vis-a-vie neighbor
always gives me
that
look
always working
at the window
the classy glassy
business woman

the rose & the virgin

Part 1: the rose

Some people are just
blessed by nature
they know how to move
they know how to look
they talk so tactfully about
every topic they touch upon
their soft and lofty
voice touches upon
and they smell like roses
even leave the rose scent on every
textile they touch
I remember how my bed smelled after
she left
previously the blanket was stiff from the
sweat
but she turned it into a rosy creek
and her nipples like rose buds
and her lips like rose petals

Part 2: the virgin

then again some people are
less gifted but also
poison their body with their
blatant thought patterns
which have been passed to
them
without further inspection
by
society
or worse =
= their parents

I lied in bed with
a virgin
and we were
making out
and I was grabbing
her virgin
breast
her titties were
out

then I tried to get
my finger
in there
but she put it away
and said "NO"
and that means no
obviously
I asked her
if she wanted
to pet my
dick but she made
a grimace which
oozed of disgust

like we weren't
just animals

then
she continued
kissing me
but I wasn't in
the mood
to suck on lips
or letting my lips
be sucked
so we just
lied
beside
each other

the whole time
there was a smell
a fishy smell
that smelly smell
and it got
worse and
worse
it smelled like the
younger
more potent
aggressive
stinging
biting
far more revolting
adolescent of my
old mans hyper manly
sweat
only when she left I
got aware
of that smell
in the room

on my face
and I washed my lips
and I washed my fingers
and I washed them thoroughly
but the smell
wouldn't go away
and I smelled it
everytime I
moved my face
everytime I
moved my lips

I thought it
wouldn't go away
That I'd never be
freed of it
I thought this
might be a curse
my curse
I thought it
was the time
to be finally and
ultimately
punished
for my sins

but everything has
an end :)

sometime

in the bus on the way to get my charger

at approximately half past 7 or 9
I opened my eyes for
the first time today

"It's too early" I thought
equally delighted and disturbed
about my well-restedness

Now it's maybe 10 am
(I don't have my phone with me)

midmorning/forenoon I have an appointment
to buy a book
only now I realize my misconception
midmorning/forenoon isn't just 11 am
it also could be earlier

Kawasaki sperm

incognito
incocknito
in cock nut o

bukkake
bukkake
salvation

the new baptism
baptized in
Kawasaki sperm

strengthen
purify
forgive sins
hot dog period blood

period blood ketchup
hot dog

red light
white spirit
ecstasy

pain killer

a new being is born

strengthen foreskin
purify vulva

black night
red light
black sky
Kawasaki sperm

speaking with my father

My father looked at me
with this this-young-adult-
was-once-a-sperm-in-my-
nutsack-and-now-I-can-
have-a-full-blown-conversation-
with-him-look

kinda proud
and incredulous

abstractly amused
grinning

cemetery

What do you think
when you see a cemetery?

"Wow, who transported all
that stone?"

"Who dug all the graves
for the corpses?"

"Who has already formed an
emotional relationship
with the stone as it
represents the loved one?"

"Who sees a cemetery
and wants his corps to
selfishly occupy land
without existing?"

"Why doesn't it seem
like death at all?"

Or do you do the math
and think
"Damn, there lies the
body that accumulated
76 years of human
consciousness but
now isn't anymore"

studying

I was again there
Doing something very
Important
For university
Now that I'm
A student

And she said
"alright, I'm not gonna
Bother you"
But guess
What
She did

Standing there
walking behind me
Searching for
Something
Ending up
Sitting
In my
Lap
It's always
Like a cat
Always
I couldn't think of anything
Other than a
Cat

And Judith butler
Would be super
Mad
Right now
But I'm
Not Judith
Butler

And in that moment
I wished that
Kim jung un
Or a general of his
Who maybe lost
His shit
Or a bet
Drunk on north
Korean beer
Or something
Dropped the h bomb
Right there
To end it on a high

But as you read these
Lines it means
That he did not
And I try to relive these
Moments as romantic
Memories
Writing vague words
About it

random impact

HOW COULD THAT NOISE
THAT MAYBE SOUNDED
LIKE A WORD
PENETRATE MY MIND
AND SUFFOCATE MY
　FREE FLOATING THOUGHTS

HOW COULD THAT COME
OUT OF A MOUTH
OUT OF NOTHING —
　YET NON-EXISTENCE

AND VANISH WITH ALL
I THOUGHT WAS
　　INSIDE ME ?

contradiction

If you think that you're
a simp
you will show anti - simp
behaviour

to compansate it

If you think that you're
unmanly
you will act super manly
     to compensate it

If you think that you're
boring (inside)
you will make your outside
flashy
to compensate it

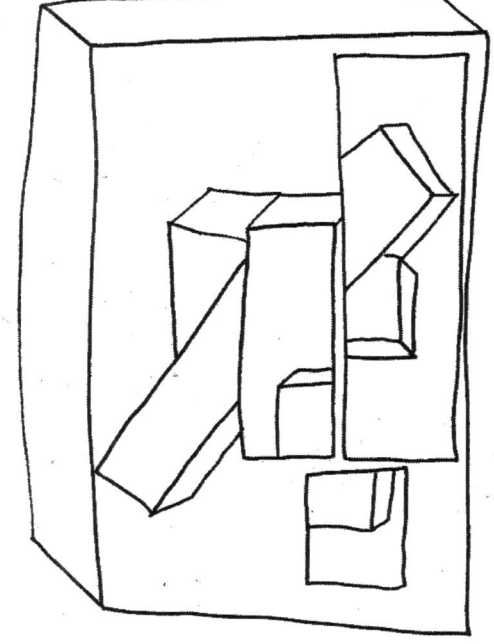

the longest night of the year

Today we have the
longest night of the year but
my phone is nearly
dead and it vibrated
drenched in a message

for a moment I mistook myself
for the
message from the person
it was the idea, the imagination
of someone saying something
never said

I played along and thought
of myself as the
mirror I can mirror myself in
and this was pleasing
as it would confine my
existence in a mirror
to a mirror
it is the symbol of myself

and the message(s) went something like:
"If you don't come, I'm dating someone else today"
"I don't know what you want. My battery is dead
and I'm cold. I'm going home"
"I'm tired of games"
"congratulations. you fooled me. I hope you're happy
-
I wish you all the best"

it was the perfect piece of fiction
taking place in reality and I accidentally
found myself being the
protagonist

all I'm left with is
myself (as always luckily)
and irony = the freedom
to avoid yourself

oops I meant sarcasm

TIC TAC... TOE

BEFORE SHE CAME
I STARED AT THE
CEILING

AND DREAMED UP
A NEW PERSONA
FOR ME

BUT I DECIDED TO BE
NOTHING

AND THAT IS MYSELF

colours

For a moment
I focused on the silence
it became so loud
The dead walls were
           screaming

It was fleeting
(it = the [it] in everything)
But it wasn't lost
Just not here
anymore
peaceful

(These words mix
idea of experience
with the vague
certainty of an
impression on an
imaginary crowd
to top it off with the
inherent/automatic
self-asserting
self-projection)

highway romance

You & me
We were in the
milky way
Wasting our time
Tasting our genitals

You & me
We were listening
to your music
It was ok
No really it wasn't bad

You & me
Jeopardizing
the other highway
users
Because you
undressed
and showed
me your tits

the fauteuil

and when a friend decided to
indicate a real conversation
about honest feelings and trust
and the mimic started to tune in
displaying what we've learned in
movies
I asked myself how real this
might be (?)
but that might be a question
of belief
everything is real
if you think it
and don't doubt it

romance is a hollywood product
and sells
sells roses and marriage
but do drug dealers in new york
get influenced by movies
displaying drug dealers??????
or did the drug dealers
influence the movies????
they go hand in hand
they must go hand in hand
because everything goes hand in hand
but it still means that the actor
sets the benchmark for reality

silence with each other

I SAID TO HER
"WE GET ALONG WELL
WHEN WE DON'T TALK"

AND SHE LAUGHED

BUT ONLY BECAUSE
IT WAS TRUE

extra

RELIGION IS
CAPITALIZED
SPIRITUALITY

Money

I live in capitalism
everything I do
is an investment

Everything is a product
and has it's worth
which makes it
comparable......

How much am I gonna
invest in a partner

??????????????

a year?
my sexual freedom?
was it a good deal?
I wanna buy a 2nd life!

New year New me

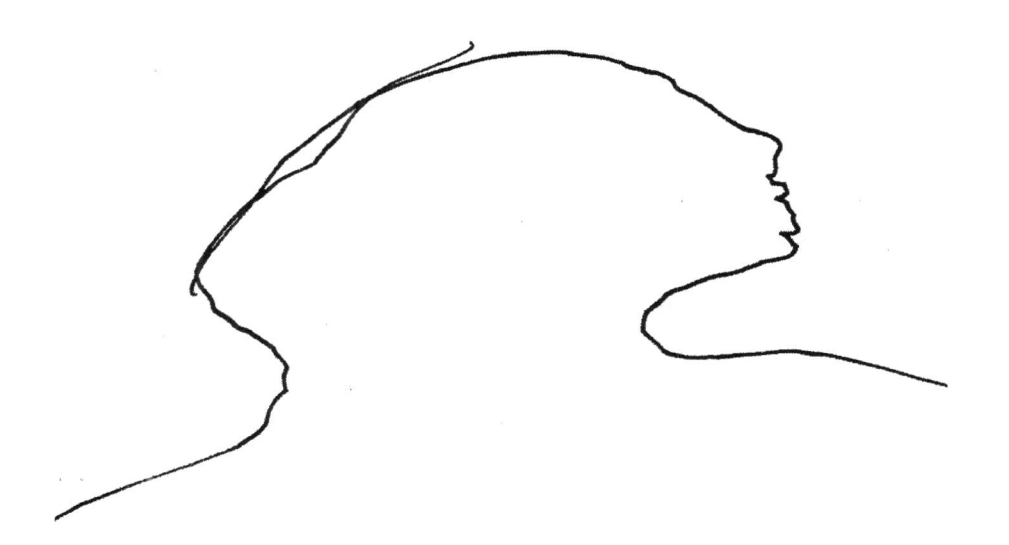

high in school

yes the second time
I was high in
school
one of the two fuckups
who eventually didn'
t
finish the school
brought a bong to school
a very small
tiny
bong

and we had 10 minutes
to hit it
but i didn't like the bong
judged by it's shape
but also was terrified
appalled
by what I was about to witness
the aggressive bubbling
the excessive coughing
the faces they made
the faces

so I sticked to the joint
instead
but it took time
(inexperienced and young)
and when I was finished
(they waited for me)
(they were basically
retardedly paralized)
they decided to go home

But I
went to class
and was 14 minutes late
and the teacher said
„Oh, you decided to come?
I already registered you as missing"
(in the class book)
but i was too high to dare
to just leave the class
so i just waited for the class
to end

> silence ended in reciprocal agreement
> without being stated as something
> wordly things should describe

    no please
I don't want your
cheap sex anymore
I finally found some meaning
I found a treasure
between her legs
so bright that
I turn off the light
when it shines
so bright that
I put on sunglasses
when it shines
so bright that
I forgot

Maybe I'll come
back someday
to redeem my
ticket
but I gotta roll
gotta ride the wave
as long as I
can feel
differ
wrong from
right

so keep these sinful
offers away
or hurl them in my
face
it doesn't matter
because
I - Don't - Care
i am a human now

GUILT

Cash Money Poem

Sometimes my thoughts
are so loud
that I can't see

We are so deep
with our thoughts

But even bus drivers
　　　　have deep thoughts
But no platform
　　no interest
　　　to share
Maybe self-sufficient
　　and self-confident

But what does the
„even" say about
　　　our superficial
　　　　judgement?
Putting people in
boxes because
they do the
crucial work for
us

Is this how we
thank our parents
working normal jobs
to give us the
resources to think
of them as
　　　idiots?

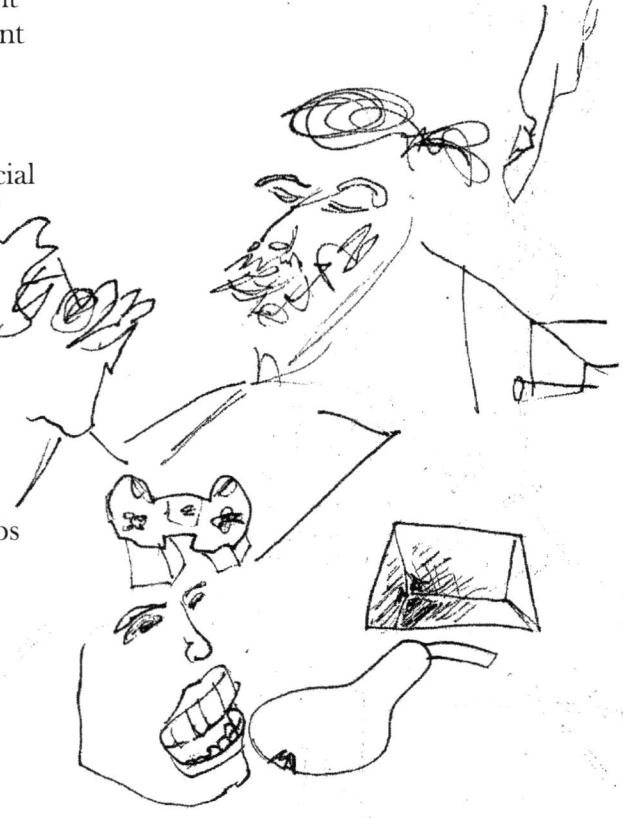

baby producing process simulation accident

We simulated the baby producing process
And the key moment is
To pull the magic sausage out
Before it explodes into salty organic glue
But this time
Something like a ghost
Or a god
Held my magic wand
In the love box

I was panicking
And sucked the sperm out
Of the vagina
But it didn't work
It was like chalk on a chalk board

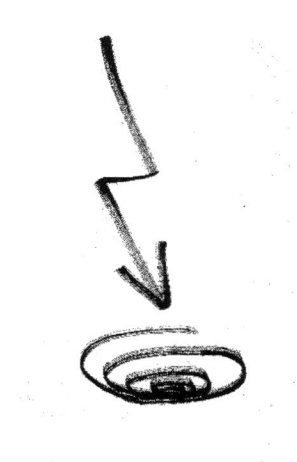

The holistic approach

After she soaked
my carpet in beer
(my precious carpet)
(three times)
and kissed my lips
and subtly stroked
my penis

she left

and I was left
naked in my room
with myself

But you don't understand.....
before sex gets infected
with mind games it's better
to stick with masturbation

Sex is the last
animal thing left
in human life

and even sex is
mainly motivated
by phantasy

But deliberately
using sex for
the power over
sex is

ABSurd
ABStraction

Call it ABS-Syndrom

Sunscreen*

Some people are genuinly
interested in your
     well being
and their childish eyes
     tell it

Others ask you about
     your life
and every word
is wrong
is a mosquito bite
in the ego

and they talk so easy
and condescending about
morals
wishing to impose
them on you
Because they're
half assing their
lifes away

and they get
even madder
when it's not working

your brain-soul
was blocking
the shade
standing in the
sunlight
without sun-cream

But I feel pity
it's just suffering
on a shallow level

at the metro

At the metro
the human I was talking to
was balancing its body weight
on the outside of its feet
and I was worried about its ankles
so I asked the human if it was
feeling nervous or anxious
and the nervousness turned
into anger
So I said something about coitus
and its mother
to make the anger vulgar
and to make the human
comfortable again

experiences shape the mind

Have you ever seen
a porn
Involving a human
    and a horse?

The prepubescent
brain is very susceptible
to the possible

Have you ever heard
a kid cry on acid?

Sanity goes hand in hand
with a graspable notion
of outside reality

animals and humans in comparison

GIRAFFES WOULD ROLL
   IF THEY COULD

CHIMPANZEES WOULD SPEAK
   IF THEY COULD

I WIPE MY ASS
   WITH TOILET PAPER

superstition

TODAY I MASTURBATED
AND THOUGHT OF YOU

NOW I'M SECRETLY
HOPING AND TERRIFIED
TO SEE YOU
AROUND EVERY CORNER
I WALK PAST

a political dream (utopy)

I had a dream
i saw a fistfight breaking out
between jesus and allah
before they jumped at
each other
jesus said: „YOU ARE
JUST A LITTLE FAKER; YOU
ARE A PUSSY ASS FAKER BOI"
and allah or mohammed I'm not
quite sure screamed back
at him: „YOU'RE MOTHER WAS
A WHORE AND YOU'RE DAD
THOUGHT SHE IS A VIRGIN"
and jesus just countered:
(and I thought this was brilliant)
„ YOUR * "

and after hearing a few bones
crash into flesh and skin
marx appeared out of nowhere
and pulled jesus away
and pushed him back
and stood in front of allah

both stood in awe
pure silence
unfiltered silence

then marx spoke:
„he who preaches peace
is the one who needs it
the most.
trust me
I know what I'm talking
about"
and they lived
happily
ever
after

religion

Today I went to buy a boudrillard
and they wished me good luck
but I've already read some lefebvre
in english
so I'll be okay, I said

coming up from the underground metro
at *Naschmarkt*
I set eyes upon the *Jugendstil* buildings
and immediatly fell unto my knees
and stretched out on the ground
and kissed the ground
overwhelming
not worthy
grateful

the homeless guy gave me
a look
disdainful
but he is not wrong
I would hate the asphalt too
If I was exposed
to it
day
and
night

When I was 14 I had to shoot a dog

It was in poor albania
It was a rich mans dog
The beast had gone
Mad
Gone Wild
With saliva as thick as sperm
Dangling from his loud teeth

He was as big as the granny
He was about to rip apart
And I shot him in self defense
Self defense for the granny
The bullet turned a life off
Turned it off
Like the light in a room

But seeing life
Go away
The air reverberating
Slowly becoming silent again
I can tell
That life isn't included
In the body

Imaginary conversation with butter

Hello butter
I would have asked you something
if I could

I'd like to know
Why I can still see her naked
with her fine nipples
and fine breast
and fine eyes
and fine features
fine face in general
and also very elegant
but I'm getting off the point

I merely wonder
That I
Still have
The picture
in front of me
it's strange
unusual
but who knows how long this lasts

Also I've thought
about a principle
a thought experiment so to say
Oh one should take his time for everything
Repeat everything till you understand it
never mind short digression over

so:
when a human reflects himself
and then judges his reflection
then he could go one step further
and reflect the position of the reflection
and then always reflect about that
he could never reach
the core of absolute reflection
because there still is a remainder of reminiscence
a feeling which
stains
stains
stains
stains
an endless moment
through the endless reflection
but only inside
is it therefore useless??

some words to my dad in english that he will never read but i make him feel with my actions in his presence

thank you dad for slapping the shit outta
my face when I was younger
and I mean that because
maybe it wasn't the best method but I
know that no human really wants
to hurt any other human so
I can tell that you have a heart of gold
in your hard shell and I know
that last time you walked in on us
watching some dipshit movie
that you cried like a bitch that your
eyes weren't tearing from the cold but I
dig that and i dig that you didn't want
us to know cus that makes you who
you are and gives us the opportunity
to learn from you
and I know it wasn't entirely your fault
cus with the dictator and not having
a dad in old communist albania a
boy has to prove some things so
it is very okay because at the end of the
day everyone would have done
the same things if one was in your
skin the entire time

Peer pressure and standardization

The guy from migos (offset)
grabbed his wife's butt (cardi b)
he could feel
just subtly
the silicone crunching
and in an unlucky moment
it popped
and it smelled like a dog
had shat his soul out

He was lucky enough
to perceive this
as a metaphor
It looked good from outside
the symbol of fertility
but inside
it was just plastic

(this piece of work is entirely fictional so please don't sue me)

dancing in the moon light

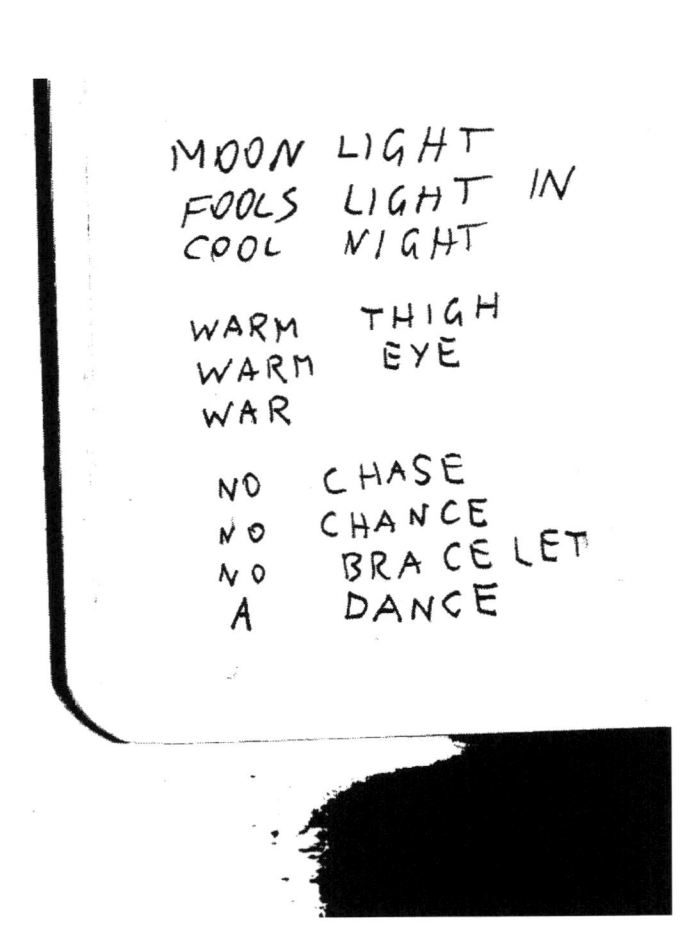

MOON LIGHT
FOOLS LIGHT IN
COOL NIGHT

WARM THIGH
WARM EYE
WAR

NO CHASE
NO CHANCE
NO BRACELET
A DANCE

In a room

In a room
With a few drops of wine
And a few pairs of lips
The happening is quite fragile
If you push it
It might break

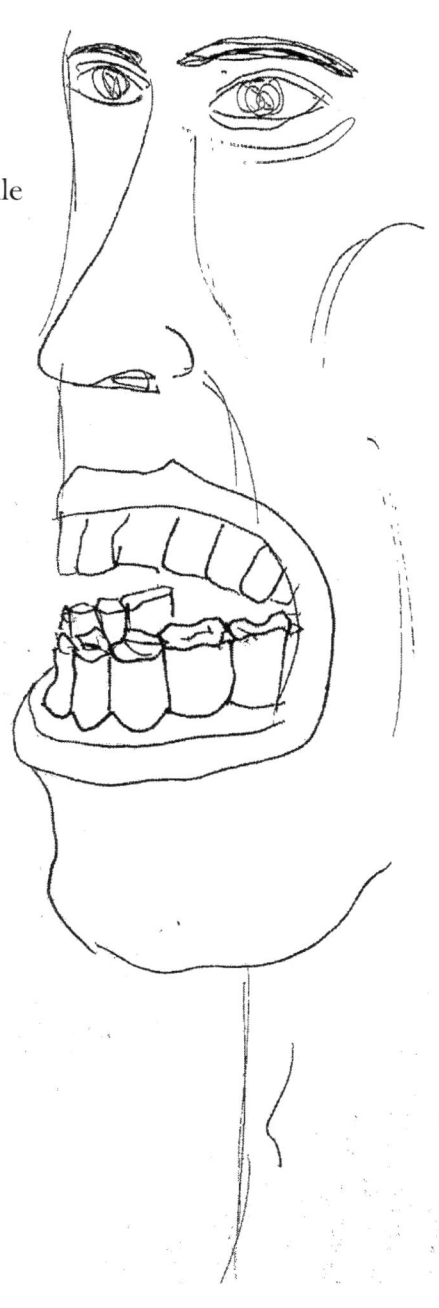

Love

It's always a special feeling
When your girlfriend tells you
That a guy confessed his
Love for her

A very tragical
And comical scene
I picture

And it shows the mechanics of love
And the value of love

But do they know that the girlfriends
Tell this to their boyfriends?

Hate (projected from the inside outside)

Did you know that the
Great „le corbusier"
Was ready to gag mussolinis
Fascistic cock
Just to have his dream
Palace and
His ideal of the city
Realized?

Furthermore I am 100%
Sure that hitler would've
Sucked 25 jewish dicks
To gain
World power and
Domination
Because hate is never reasonable
It is a passion

Why else would he give
His soldiers speed
And brag about the
Superiority of the aryans

The crying episode

When she unlocked the door
I saw her sitting on the floor
Beside the toilette

I sat right next to her
On the cold tiles
Till the hemorrhoids sprout
Out my ass
Like mushrooms
And busted
While I caught every tear
Of hers
With my fingertip

the worst thing

THE WORST THING IS
TO SEE
HOW SOME PEOPLE
TREAT THEMSELVES

Don't throw this away!

NICE CONNECTION
WHEN BOTH CUM
AT THE SAME TIME

PLAYBOY GOT SHOT
TOYBOY GOT PAID
LOVER GOT LOVED

DON'T THROW THIS
AWAY!

How beautiful

How beautiful
we still have so many
years to waste

How sad that our
parents are going
to die one day

Histories may be forgotten

Just get on stage and say
„life is suffering"
and you may become
happy
in moments like this

The suffering is the
price I pay
otherwise life wouldn't cost
anything
and wouldn't be worth
anything

Pro-tip:
use babywipes
to limit suffering

Printed in Great Britain
by Amazon